# THE MINSTREL'S DAUGHTER

LINDA SMITH

# THE MINSTREL'S DAUGHTER

*Book One of the* TALES *of* THREE LANDS *trilogy*

COTEAU BOOKS
WWW.COTEAUBOOKS.COM

Edited by Barbara Sapergia.
Cover painting by Stella East.
Cover and book design by Duncan Campbell.
Printed and bound in Canada by Transcontinental Printing.

**Library and Archives Canada Cataloguing in Publication**

Smith, Linda, 1949-
The minstrel's daughter / Linda Smith.

(Tales of three lands ; 1)
ISBN 1-55050-309-X

I. Title.  II. Series: Smith, Linda, 1949-  Tales of three lands ; 1.

PS8587.M5528M46 2004          jC813'.54          C2004-905188-1


10   9   8   7   6   5   4   3   2

*Available in Canada & the US from:*
Fitzhenry and Whiteside
2517 Victoria Avenue            195 Allstate Parkway
Regina, Saskatchewan            Markham, Ontario
Canada   S4P 0T2                Canada   L3R 4T8

The publisher gratefully acknowledges the financial assistance of the Saskatchewan Arts Board, the Canada Council for the Arts, the Government of Canada through the Book Publishing Industry Development Program (BPIDP), and the City of Regina Arts Commission, for its publishing program.

*To my family, my best and most devoted fans.*

# FINDING SPELL

THE WIZARD'S HOUSE WAS TALL AND NARROW, like the wizard himself. Its top floor leaned forward over the street, just as Master Weaver leaned forward from long years of bending to hear what shorter people had to say. Cat stood in front of the house and chewed her lip.

It wasn't that she was frightened of Master Weaver. She had known him most of her life, if only slightly, and he had always had a kind word and a slow smile for her, as for all children. And she had the money to pay him. She clutched the three silver coins in her pocket.

But how would he react to her request? Would he refuse to cast the spell? Worse: would he tell her mother?

Cat scowled. Why did she have to live in a place where nothing was private? Everyone in the village of Frey-under-Hill and on the farms that stretched out beyond it knew her and her family. The Ashdales of Ashdale Farm had been here for generations. Sometimes, Cat thought that everyone in Frey-under-Hill was rooted, like trees, in its soil.

She wandered across the cobblestoned road that served the hamlet as its main, and only, street, and stood on the far side, gazing down tall cliffs to the River Frey below. What would it be like to travel all the way upriver to busy Freyfall, or even past it to Freybourg, where Queen Elira made her home? What would it be like to go beyond Freya's borders, to cross the Rim Mountains into Uglessia, or to go downstream to Frey-by-the-Sea and sail over the ocean to the fabled isles of Islandia?

Well, maybe she'd find out. Soon. Raising her chin, she pulled her heavy tawny hair away from her face. She waited till a cart passed, then marched back across the road and knocked firmly on the wizard's door.

After a moment, a short, apple-cheeked woman with greying brown hair opened it. "Catrina! What brings you here?"

Cat cleared her throat. "I would like to see Master Weaver, please, Mistress Fowler."

The housekeeper's welcoming smile faded. "No trouble, I hope. Is anything wrong at the farm? Your grandparents...?"

"They're fine."

"Thank Freyn for that. Winnona and Caleb Ashdale are fine folk. Sturdy, too, but they *are* getting on. We're all doing that, mind."

"They're fine," Cat repeated.

"And your mother? There's naught amiss with the wedding plans, I trust."

Cat's face stiffened. "No."

"Good. She's fortunate to be marrying a kind man like Kenton Herd. I was chatting with your Aunt Dalia just yesterday, and she said the whole family is so pleased."

Cat's hands clenched. "May I see Master Weaver, please."

Mistress Fowler hesitated. "He's busy. If there's naught amiss —"

"I have the coins to pay."

"Bless you, child, it's not that. But I hate to disturb him if it's not important."

"It *is* important. It's private," Cat added as the housekeeper opened her mouth.

There was a brief silence. Cat held her breath.

"Very well," the woman said. Her voice had cooled. Then she looked up at the sky and her tone warmed. "Best come in anyway. It looks like rain. Follow me."

Cat trailed her through the hall, which smelled of soap and baking bread, and up four flights of well-scrubbed stairs. The housekeeper knocked at a door on the top floor.

"Come in," called a deep, soft voice.

Mistress Fowler opened the door. "Mistress Catrina Ashdale to see you, sir. She says it's important."

"Catrina. Do come in." Master Vail Weaver rose from his chair, flexing his tall, lanky frame as though he'd been sitting too long. He smiled kindly at Cat.

The window behind him gave a clear view of the dark clouds that had gathered above the street and the cliffs beyond. The grey light that filtered in showed Cat papers and books everywhere: stacked in neat piles on the floor,

3

piled on chairs, and strewn across a large pinewood table.

"I'm sorry to disturb you. I know you're busy."

His laugh sounded like distant, rumbling thunder. "I am indeed. I'm trying to remember bits and pieces of magic that I've learned – and forgotten – over the years."

"Master Weaver will be attending a wizards' council in Freyfall later this spring," Mistress Fowler announced proudly. "All the best wizards in Freya will be there."

"As well as wizards from Islandia and Uglessia," Master Weaver added. "I'll be leaving in a week's time for Frey-by-the-Sea for a preliminary meeting with Kerstin Brooks and a delegation from Islandia, then sailing with them to Freyfall."

Cat swallowed. She knew, of course – everyone in Frey-under-Hill knew – that their wizard had been apprenticed as a young man to the father of the great Kerstin Brooks. But for him to meet with her, with other important wizards...

"I'm sorry. I didn't mean...I didn't know you were so busy. I'll go."

"Nonsense. I'm never too busy to help. Anyway, an interruption will do me good. Here. Sit." He removed some papers from a chair, nodded dismissal to Mistress Fowler, and reseated himself.

Cat sat on the edge of the chair.

"What can I do for you, Catrina?" He folded his hands on the table and leaned forward.

"I... How much does a finding spell cost?" Surely the three coins in her pocket, carefully gathered, carefully hoarded, were enough.

The wizard's light eyes were intent on her face. "Well," he said slowly, "that would depend. What had you thought of offering?"

"Three silver coins."

"A princely sum," he said gravely. "I think two coins would be adequate. What is it you wish me to find? Some prized possession you've mislaid?"

"No."

He waited. She fidgeted, wishing he'd look away. The silence dragged on.

She took a deep breath. "I want you to find my father."

"Your father!" The wizard's bushy white eyebrows shot up.

She gulped. "Yes."

A small frown creased his forehead. "That might be difficult."

"Why?" Cat's voice shook.

"Well...it must be a number of years since he's been around here."

"Twelve years."

He nodded. "And never for long when he *was* here, I understand. Impressions of him would be very faint indeed. And I never met him. Can you describe him?"

Could she? She squeezed her eyes shut. "He's tall." But was he? Everyone was tall to a three-year-old. "He has yellow hair." She remembered how it gleamed in the sun. "He laughed a lot. Even his voice laughed." She opened her eyes. "I'm sorry."

He sighed. "It's not very much. Do you have anything that belonged to him?"

Her face brightened. "Yes." She dug into her pocket and pulled out a small, dented tin whistle. "Here."

He took it and studied it thoughtfully. "Your father was a minstrel, I understand."

"*Is* a minstrel," she corrected.

"Is? You have recent word of him, then?"

"No." She bent her head, her heavy hair swinging forward to hide her face.

He waited, then asked mildly, "But you're sure he's still a minstrel?"

"He loves music. He loves it more than anything." More than Mother. More than me.

"I see."

She tensed, waiting for the scornful words, the accusing words, the words she had heard all too often. Words about wandering musicians, words about men with no sense of responsibility. But all he said was, "You must have inherited your gift from him, then. I hear you have a beautiful voice."

She flushed. "Thank you."

He examined the whistle again. "This should help. But Catrina..."

"What?"

"I don't know whether I should cast this spell for you."

She raised angry hazel eyes to his face. "Why not?"

He hesitated. "Why do you want to find your father?" he asked at last.

"Because he's my father. Isn't it only natural that I want to discover where he is, how he is?"

"Yes, but... Why do you want to find him *now?*"

She looked away.

She felt his eyes on her face. Finally he said quietly, "Kenton Herd is a good man."

"I'm sick and tired of everyone telling me that!" She heard the shrillness in her voice and stopped, appalled. "I...I'm sorry," she stammered.

"It's all right."

"Anyway, that's not why... It has nothing to do with the wedding. And even if I did want to find my father, I couldn't, could I – not in person, that is. I don't have the money."

"No," he said slowly. After a moment he added, "Kenton will be glad to have you as a daughter, I am sure."

She said nothing, just looked at him.

He sighed. "Very well. I will try."

Holding the whistle in one large hand and staring at it intently, he uttered the spell. Some of the words were unfamiliar, but most were ordinary enough, though oddly patterned. Nevertheless, Cat shivered, as though cold fingers were running up and down her spine. Never in her fifteen years had she been so close to power.

The wizard was very still. Cat found she was holding her breath and let it out carefully, not wanting to break the silence. She watched the lined, intent face while the clouds beyond the window thickened and blackened.

The chair was hard. She started to shift, then made herself sit quietly.

She waited.

Finally, the wizard stirred. He looked at her and smiled.

She leaned forward eagerly. "Did the spell work?"

"It did. I found him."

"Where is he?"

"I saw him first in a room, a small, shabby room. Playing a lute. I think someone else was there, though I'm not sure. Then I saw him strolling down a busy street. That's all."

"That's all? But...did you recognize the street?"

"No."

"But you said you found him!"

He smiled again. "I heard the boom of a waterfall."

She stared at him for a moment. Then recognition dawned. "Freyfall!"

He nodded.

A slow smile spread over her face. "Thank you," she said softly. She fumbled in her pocket and produced two coins.

"You are most welcome." He accepted the money and returned the whistle, then rose, a bit stiffly, and accompanied her to the door. "Catrina..."

"Yes?"

He seemed to be choosing his words with care. "Change is sometimes hard to accept. But give this marriage of your mother's a chance."

He had no right. No right to assume he knew how she felt. Cat's hands jammed into fists. Then her anger faded before fear.

"You won't tell anyone, will you? Why I came?"

He looked at her soberly. "I think you should tell your mother. But no, I will not tell anyone. That would be breaking one of the laws of wizardry."

She sighed with relief. "Well, thank you again," she said awkwardly.

"Freyn shed His light upon you, child." He watched her all the way down the four flights of stairs.

Emerging into the grey afternoon, Cat took a deep breath. She had done it.

Done what? She knew where her father was now, but she was no closer to finding him – *really* finding him. Freyfall was far away and, as she had told Master Weaver, she had no money.

Slowly, she walked across the road and stood at the edge of the cliff, looking down. Narrow steps, cut into the face of the rock, led to a wharf below. Boats stopped there briefly on their way up and down the river, but passage on them was expensive. As for walking...even if she could, it would take weeks. Months. And Gayland Bellmore was not a man to stay long in one place. He got restless.

A drop of rain fell on her head. Reluctantly, Cat turned away from the river, back to the long line of buildings that stretched along the clifftop, and the green fields that lay beyond. She would get soaked, but she should hurry home anyway. She had nowhere else to go.

# WEDDING GIFT

"WILL YOU SING FOR US AT THE WEDDING, CAT?"

Cat stopped pushing her food around the plate, but didn't glance up. "Sing?"

"It would be a beautiful gift, the best we could have."

Cat looked at her mother then. Lianna was leaning forward, the lace collar on her good navy dress catching the evening light. A tendril of fair hair had escaped from its bun onto her cheek. She was smiling, but her grey eyes were anxious. "Will you?" she repeated.

*She really wants me to. For the first time in six months, what I do matters to her.* Wordlessly, Cat nodded.

"Good," Kenton Herd said heartily. "I've heard so much about what a lovely voice you have." He smiled at her, his blue eyes crinkling with pleasure. She forced a stiff smile to her own lips before returning her attention to her meal.

The meal deserved attention. All day, the house had been

filled with the smells of roasting lamb, mint sauce, and baking bread, and Aunt Dalia had brought some of her prized delicacies, including the honey cakes Cat loved. But she had little appetite, even for honey cakes. All through dinner, she'd toyed with her food, using it as an excuse to avoid joining in the talk and laughter.

No one would hear me anyway, Cat thought. Not with all the noise. She glanced around. The extra tables they'd brought in were all crowded. Cat felt as though her home had been invaded. She looked at her grandmother, but Winnona's eyes were sparkling. Pink bloomed in her cheeks as though she were a girl, not a sixty-two-year-old grandmother. Cat sighed.

Kenton had four brothers and three sisters, and they had all come to the gift giving, and brought their wives or husbands and wagonloads of children with them. How different from her family! There was only herself, her mother, her grandparents, her widowed aunt, and her cousin. Small as it was, Cat wished it were even less well represented. Aunt Dalia had a critical eye and a sharp tongue. As for her son... Cat shot a sideways glance at her cousin Morty, two years her senior. At least he was too busy eating to send any of his sly, smirking smiles her way.

"How are your crops coming, Caleb?" Kenton asked. He undid the top button of his formal shirt and rolled up his sleeves, as though ready to plunge his hands into the dirt of his own farm.

Cat's grandfather leaned back in his chair. A ray of sunlight slanted in through the window to gild his lean, weathered face. "Fine. If we get a bit more rain than we have the last few years, we'll have a good yield. I've got most of the planting done – with Cat's help. She's a great worker. I don't know what I'll do without her." He smiled at Cat.

She smiled back. She had always loved working with her quiet, patient grandfather, loved, too, the work itself: the feel of rich black earth on her hands, the look of tender green shoots pushing through the ground, the touch of the early morning air as she walked the cows to pasture. She would miss all that. Her eyes misted.

"Cat can still help you, Father – perhaps stay here at seeding and harvest times."

Cat's eyes snapped to her mother's face, then away. Her mother needn't sound *that* eager to get rid of her.

"That won't be necessary," Dalia said. Heads turned her way. She cleared her throat. "I thought we'd move in here, now that Lianna and Cat are leaving. You'll need my help in the house, Mother, and Morty can be a big help on the farm – more than Cat ever was."

"But what about the blacksmith shop?" Caleb asked.

Dalia shrugged. "I can sell it easily enough. The journeyman's eager to buy, and he can pay me off gradually. It's been a heavy burden, ever since my dear Morris died." Her plump fingers plucked the black-rimmed handkerchief she always carried from the breast pocket of her maroon dress, and dabbed her eyes and doughy cheeks. "And Morty should learn more about the farm since it will be his some day."

"But –" Cat began, then stopped. She had never really thought about it, but always, at the back of her mind, there had been the assurance that, sometime in the future – the very distant future, she hoped – the farm would be hers. Morty had his father's blacksmith shop, after all.

She looked at her grandfather. Surely he would deny Aunt Dalia's claim. But Caleb was looking at his wife. The two of them exchanged a long glance, then Winnona rose. Some of the sparkle had left her eyes, and the pink had faded from her cheeks.

"We'll talk more about this later. Now is the time for gift giving." She led the way into the large parlour, where a fire burned in the hearth, despite the mildness of the spring evening. Thick stone walls kept the house cool, even in the heat of summer.

Cat trailed after the others, entering the room as the children, who had eaten out in the yard under the supervision of the older ones, came running in. At least she hadn't been relegated to eat with them, Cat thought as she sank onto the floor. The chairs were all occupied.

There were gifts for everyone. Lianna distributed hers first, small presents for every member of Kenton's family: sweets for the children, embroidered handkerchiefs and bottled jams and jellies for the adults.

Then it was Kenton's turn to give gifts to Lianna's family. He handed Winnona, Caleb, Dalia, and Morty theirs, then looked around. "Cat?"

A crowd of children stood in front of her, hiding her as they gaped at the presents. Cat grimaced, wishing she could remain hidden. Slowly, she rose and walked forward.

Kenton reached into the sack beside him and drew

something out. "I saw this when I was in Frey-by-the-Sea a couple of months back. I thought it was something you might like." He held it out. Wonderingly, she touched it with a tentative finger, then took it in her hand.

It was a flute, made of the finest wood and inlaid with pictures of small woodland creatures, peering out from under leaves and behind vines.

"Thank you," she whispered, raising her eyes to Kenton's face. It was a broad, blunt-featured face, currently wearing an anxious frown. The frown evaporated when he saw her expression. For a moment, they gazed at one another.

"Play it," one of the smaller children begged.

Cat shook her head. This was not the right place. Tomorrow morning, she would take the flute to the small hill that overlooked the farm, and greet the sun with its song.

"A fine choice," Lianna said softly, taking Kenton's hand in her own.

"Now perhaps you'll throw away that old tin whistle," Dalia said.

Cat stiffened. "No."

"No indeed," Winnona agreed quickly. "And now that we've finished with the other gifts, we shall present the bride-and-groom-to-be with theirs."

Cat watched from behind her screen of hair as gift after gift was given, amidst exclamations and laugher. There were woven blankets, embroidered sheets, homemade preserves, rag rugs. Cat had embroidered two pillow slips, working at them with dogged, if impatient, determination. She eyed the elegant embroidery on the other gifts as she presented her own offering, accepted the couple's smiling thanks, then slunk back to her corner.

Two of Kenton's brothers disappeared, to return bearing a large carved wooden clothes chest. Beaming, they placed it before the bridal pair.

"It's beautiful," Lianna cried.

It was. Made of polished oak and carved with the decorated initials L and K, its clean, pure lines sang.

Kenton cleared his throat. "Not bad, brothers," he said gruffly.

They grinned. "We've waited so long for you to get married that we thought a special effort was called for," one of them said.

Kenton grinned too. "But see what I get for waiting – a perfect gift and a perfect bride."

Dalia's voice cut through the laughter like a sharp knife through tender roast lamb. "It's too bad you didn't wait too, Lianna, instead of taking up with the first irresponsible wanderer who came along with a handsome face and a pretty song."

Morty's snicker died in the embarrassed silence.

Cat's face flamed. She rose, fists clenched. "How can you –"

Lianna quelled her with a look. Laughter had fled from her face, like horses from a threatening storm, but her voice was controlled.

"I don't regret 'taking up' with Gayland, as you call it."

"Not regret it? Well, you might not mind having a child out of wedlock and having a man desert you, but what about the rest of the family? You don't deserve –" She glanced at Kenton and broke off. Red splotches marked her face like an unhealthy rash.

Lianna was on her feet, her own face heated. "Don't you take your bitterness out on me! Don't –"

"Lianna." Winnona's voice was low but firm.

Lianna looked at her mother, then took a deep breath. When she spoke again, her voice was calmer. "I loved Gayland, but I couldn't marry him. We were too different. And he didn't desert me. We parted when I realized I could no longer face a wandering life on the road, and he told me he couldn't give it up."

Cat dug her fingernails into the palms of her hands. Her throat felt tight, clogged with words she would not say, could not say, words that had lodged there for the last six months.

*It's fine for you. You're free to marry Kenton Herd. But what about me? You never thought about me when you made your decision, did you? I've had to face sniggers and sneers and pity all my life because you didn't marry Father, because you didn't love him enough to keep us together.*

Caleb's deep voice broke the awkward silence. "We must be thankful for how things turned out, Dalia. Otherwise, we wouldn't have Cat with us." He smiled at his granddaughter.

Dalia's muffled snort showed what she thought of that.

Cat sat down.

One of Kenton's brothers – Cat thought it was Brandon, but she always got them confused – cleared his throat. "We thought we'd start with the chest," he said in an obvious attempt to ease the brittle atmosphere. "After nine months or so, we'll start on a cradle." He winked at Kenton.

Laughter greeted his remark, as it was meant to do. Cat stiffened. They weren't planning to have children, were they? Weren't they too old? Surely her mother didn't want... Wasn't she enough? She glanced at her mother. Lianna's face was pink, but a small smile played around her lips.

The rest of the evening was a blur. A long blur. At last the guests straggled out into the star-filled night. Cat went in search of her mother. She found her grandmother instead.

"Do you know where Mother is?"

"In the back garden, saying farewell to Kenton. No," Winnona added, as Cat headed that way. "They need some time together."

Cat stared at her. What did she mean? Weren't they planning to spend the rest of their lives together?

"I need to talk to her."

"Not now. Maybe later, if she's not too tired. It's been a long day." Winnona yawned. She looked exhausted suddenly, the lines on her face deeper than usual.

But she and her mother always shared the last moments before bedtime, talking over the events of the day while Lianna brushed Cat's hair with slow, loving strokes.

Winnona studied her granddaughter's face. "We need to talk." She yawned again. "We'll do it in the morning."

Talk about what? About Lianna's marriage? About Dalia and Morty moving in here? About Morty having the farm, even though he would never love it as she did? About becoming Kenton's stepdaughter and forgetting her own father?

Cat turned on her heel and walked out of the kitchen, ignoring her grandmother's faint cry of protest. She went outside, not to the back where she wasn't wanted, but to the front of the house, where she stood listening to the sounds of hooves and wagon wheels fading into the night.

A warm breeze stirred the leaves of the ash trees that marched down the lane and dotted the meadows beyond. She would be leaving them soon, as she would be leaving the house, her grandparents, the little brook she could hear gurgling quietly to itself.

She would be leaving them – for what? Not for adventure, excitement, the chance to see new places and find her father. No, she would be leaving them to go to a house where she would be an unwanted, unneeded third party. Would she and her mother ever share that special time before bed again?

She clenched her hands, then winced as her right hand bit into carved edges. She had forgotten she was holding the flute. Involuntarily, her left hand moved to caress the polished wood, the curved forms of mice and squirrels, leaves and vines. Kenton had given her this. He knew her well enough to know what would give her joy, and cared enough to buy it for her. He must have spent a great deal for the flute. Perhaps...

Her breath caught. This flute was valuable. If she really wanted to leave, if she really wanted to find her father, then this flute offered her a chance, offered her passage to Freyfall.

# Voyage Begun

WILD GRASS GREW TALL BESIDE THE RIVER. Cat crouched in it, heart pounding, and waited for the mail boat. It had gone downriver five days ago. It should return today. Everyone in Frey-under-Hill knew that, for the pattern of boats going up and down Frey was part of the rhythm of their lives. A lookout was posted on top of the cliff, to call out at the first sighting.

The boat would stop only long enough to take on fresh food and water, to deliver and receive mail, and to allow passengers to embark or disembark. Freyn save her from anyone boarding today!

Would there be time for her to dash to the boat, after the last villager had left and before the boat sailed? She thought so. She hoped so. She didn't dare approach it before the townsfolk left: someone would be sure to interfere.

She shifted uneasily, and her small pack rubbed against her back. It didn't contain much, only a few changes of clothing, a bar of soap, the tin whistle, and her sole remaining coin. She clutched the flute in her hand.

Cat glanced down at the flute. For two weeks now, she had resisted playing it, afraid that if she heard it, she would find it impossible to give it up.

Once she had decided to leave, it would have been easier to go at once. But she had promised to sing at her mother's wedding, and she had kept her word.

The ache in her throat had threatened to block her song. She hadn't let it, though. The melody of "The Uniting Song" had flowed purely and clearly. Lianna's face had glowed.

Kenton had been touched too. There had been tears in his eyes when he thanked her. Again, Cat shifted uncomfortably.

They didn't need her, she reminded herself. Kenton would be relieved when he found her note. Her mother...

Yes, Lianna would grieve. And worry.

*It's her own fault. She didn't think of me when she decided to marry Kenton.*

*Anyway, I'll send word as soon as I find Father. And Mother has a new life: a new home, a new husband, perhaps, soon, a new child. She doesn't need a fifteen-year-old daughter.*

A breeze had sprung up. It rippled the tall grass around her and deposited drops of river water on her head.

The truth was, no one needed her, not even her grand-parents. Winnona and Caleb had talked it over and decided to accept Dalia's offer.

"With you and your mother gone, we'll need them

here," Winnona had said. She was sitting at the kitchen table, her normally busy hands wrapped around a mug of kala. "I can use help in the house, and your grandfather can certainly use it in the fields."

"I can come when you need me."

Caleb placed a big, dirt-stained hand over Cat's. "That's generous of you, Cat, and there's nothing I'd like better. We work together like a team of matched horses. But the truth is, I need help all the time now, not just during seeding and harvest, and so does your grandmother. We're getting on."

Cat stared down at his hand.

"That doesn't mean we won't be happy to see you, any time you can visit." Winnona's tone, usually brisk and matter-of-fact, was gentle.

Visit. But this was home. Cat looked around, at her grandparents' faces, at the whitewashed walls, the stone floor, the well-scrubbed hearth, the sunlight splashing onto the ashwood table that was the centre of the house, of their lives.

"I could live here," she blurted out.

Winnona and Caleb looked at each other. Then Winnona shook her head. "No, child. Your place is with your mother."

"It's not that we don't want you," Caleb said awkwardly. "You know we do."

Did she? Cat bent her head and studied the table. Oh, they loved her. She knew that. But they didn't need her. She didn't come first with them. She didn't come first with anyone.

"Cat..."

"It's all right." She rose. "I'd better go bring the cows in." With an effort, she kept her face serene and her steps even until she was out of sight. Then she broke down, crying and stumbling all the way to the pasture.

She'd worn a calm, untroubled mask to the wedding. She didn't want to attract anyone's scorn, anyone's pity. She'd suffered those all her life, just for being who she was. The only time her mask slipped had been when Morty had given her one of his sideways smirks and said, "I guess you'll be staying in the house now. Kenton has plenty of hired men. High time you did girl's work."

She'd turned on him. "I can do any work I want to do. I was far more use on the farm than you'll ever be." It was more than an angry boast: she might not be big, but she was quick and hard-muscled. A true cat, her grandfather said. And she knew the farm, and loved it.

"We'll see about that. Anyway, it will be my farm one day."

She had no answer for that. No answer at all.

Now here she was, crouched in the grass, her mouth dry from nervous excitement. She had left the farm – Kenton's farm – early that morning, telling her mother she would spend the day with Marthe, the daughter of the town butcher. Lianna had looked up from her baking with an absent-minded smile. "Have a good time, love." *Probably glad I'm gone,* Cat thought, walking away from the house. *She wasn't even surprised I'm spending time with Marthe, even though I've never been close to her.* Cat blinked back tears.

Once in town, she'd climbed down the steep steps in the cliff when no one was in sight. For the last two hours, she'd been kneeling or crouching here. No wonder her muscles were beginning to cramp. Cautiously, Cat shifted her position.

Then, above her head, the lookout cried, "Boat's coming!"

Cat drew back behind her screen of grass. Peering out, she saw first one, then two, then a dozen people file down the steps and wait on the pier. She could see the boat now. The breeze had died again, and the green sails were quiet in the still air. The oars flashed. People said that rowers always approached port with a brave flourish, no matter how tired they were.

One of the townsfolk turned in her direction. Cat ducked down and made herself as small as possible. She couldn't see the boat, but she heard it dock, heard shouted commands, talk, laughter, a voice calling out the names of those receiving mail, Amelia's loud laments that her sweetheart, who lived in Frey-by-the-Sea, hadn't written. How typical of Amelia. She always let everyone within hearing distance know about her woes, whether they came from midges flying into her wide-open blue eyes, or from pricking her finger as she helped her mother, the town seamstress.

Cat listened tensely. No one boarded. Her breath rushed out in a sigh of relief.

It seemed to go on forever. Cat silently cursed the cramps in her legs and the wild grass that scratched her neck. She didn't dare move.

At last, the villagers began to straggle back up the hill. Cat forced herself to wait, to remain still, until the last one had reached the top. Only then did she dare creep out of her hiding place.

A man was untying the ropes that secured the boat to the dock.

She gasped, and ran. "Wait!" She waved her arms frantically.

For a heart-plunging moment, she thought the man would ignore her. Then he turned.

"Yes?"

Cat took some more steps towards him, then stopped, her breath coming in painful pants. "I want...I want to go to Freyfall."

The sailor, a young, broad-shouldered man with curly brown hair, turned his head and called, "Captain!"

Another man, older and more formally dressed, appeared at the rail. The first sailor gestured towards Cat. "She wants to book passage to Freyfall."

The captain looked Cat over. "Can you pay?"

She flushed. True, the dress she wore was old, and crumpled from crouching – probably grass-stained too. But he needn't take that tone.

"Yes," she said haughtily. She walked closer until she was standing directly below him, and held out the flute. "Here."

His eyes narrowed. "Hmm. Let me see that."

Cat swallowed hard before reaching up to give it to him. She watched him turn it over and over in his hands, and ached to have it back.

The captain looked at her. "Where did you get this?"

"I...it's mine."

He eyed her suspiciously. "I didn't see you come down the hill with the others."

"She ran out of the grass by the river," the young sailor volunteered.

The captain's gaze sharpened. By this time, most of the rowers were frankly staring, as were the passengers, a well-dressed man and woman in early middle age and an older man, standing by himself.

"Did you steal this?" the captain barked.

"What?" Cat stared at him. Did he think she was a thief? Did all those watching eyes think...?

"No!" She flung the word at him. At them all.

The older passenger laughed. "That had the force of truth behind it," he observed.

"Hmm." The captain was still doubtful. "Not a thief, perhaps, but –. Why were you hiding?" he demanded.

Cat scrambled frantically for an answer.

"She's a runaway, that's plain," said the well-dressed woman. "She should be sent home to her parents."

"No! No, I'm not. I...I'm going to Freyfall to live with my father."

"Is that the truth?"

"Yes." Well, it was. He didn't have to know that she wasn't exactly sure where her father was.

The woman sniffed. Cat ignored her and kept her eyes fastened on the captain's face. He still looked suspicious. Then he glanced down at the flute, fingering it thoughtfully.

"All right," he said abruptly, and turned to the rowers.

"Captain, I must protest," the woman began.

He threw her an irritated frown. "Protest away. In the meantime, I have a boat to run and a schedule to keep. We've wasted enough time."

The young sailor grinned down at Cat. "Looks like you're coming." He lifted Cat bodily before she could object and plunked her on deck, then leaped aboard himself. The rowers returned to their seats. They back-paddled, then, with long, smooth strokes, headed for the middle of the river. Cat watched the buildings on top of the cliff get smaller and smaller.

The female passenger gave Cat a disapproving glare, then took her husband's arm and headed for her cabin.

Later, in her own tiny cabin, Cat lowered her pack to the floor and sank onto the cot. She had done it. She was on her way.

# FREYFALL

SHE WOULD NEVER HAVE BELIEVED A PLACE could be so big.

She had known it was a city, of course, had known it was much larger than the one long, strung-out line of buildings that was Frey-under-Hill, had known it was bigger, too, than the towns they'd passed on the trip upriver. But in all her dreams of travel, she had never imagined anything like this city, sprawled on both banks of the river and on the large island in the middle, never imagined these streets, congested with people and carts, these buildings, jammed together like so many overgrown peas in a pea pod. Never imagined this noise.

It was incredible. Deafening. First, there was the boom of the waterfall. Cat raised her eyes to the shimmering, sun-dappled wall of water that fell from a massive cliff to form foamy, swirling eddies below. The waterfall was...beautiful, Cat thought, groping for words. Magnificent. Awe-inspiring. Loud.

But it wasn't only the waterfall. It was the clopping of horse hooves, the rumble of cart and carriage wheels, the creaking of the flotilla of boats in harbour, the squawking of gulls overhead. The people.

So many people, all talking at once, all talking at the top of their lungs, or so it seemed to Cat.

How was she to find her father among so many people?

She had thought everyone in Freyfall would know, or at least know of, an accomplished musician like Gayland Bellmore. Now.... She gulped.

"Quite a place, isn't it?"

Startled, she turned to see the curly-haired rower – Rory, he was called – leaning on the railing beside her. He grinned at her. "Your first time here?"

She nodded.

"I can show you the sights, if you'd like."

He had been friendly throughout the voyage, pausing to chat whenever he was off duty and she was on deck. She'd been on deck most daylight hours, fascinated by the fields, the forests, the meadows, the towns and hamlets they passed; fascinated, too, by the river itself, in all its smooth power, in all its unexpected, turbulent twists.

"No, thank you." Rory was pleasant, but she wasn't sure she trusted him. Anyway, she wasn't here to see the sights.

He shrugged and turned to go.

"Rory..."

He turned back. "Yes?"

"If you wanted to find someone – a musician – where would you look?"

He raised surprised eyebrows, but asked no questions. "I'm not one for music myself, but there seem to be a lot of minstrels at inns and taverns, hired to entertain the guests."

"How many inns and taverns are there?"

"In Freyfall? Freyn knows. Fifty maybe. Or seventy. Or more."

She swallowed.

He'd been watching her face. "Something wrong?"

"No. No, everything's fine."

"Good. I'll be on my way, then. Freyfall awaits." He grinned and sauntered off to join a group of his fellow rowers, who were laughing and joking and clinking the new coins in their pockets. Cat watched him go, then walked slowly down the gangplank, feeling as alien as a stray sheep in a herd of cows.

It was not difficult to find either inns or taverns. They crowded around the harbour mouth like pigs at a trough. Cat wandered from one to the other, then, clutching her courage tightly, entered a large, green-shuttered inn.

She stopped on the threshold, intimidated, then moved aside hastily as a group of men pushed by her. Other customers were descending the stairs. Servants bustled by, carrying platters of food from the kitchen at the back to the crowded, noisy common room. The smell of roast duck made Cat's stomach gurgle. It was dinnertime.

"Can I help you?" A man with a shiny, balding head and a round belly had stopped in front of her.

"Oh! Oh, yes, thank you. I was wondering... I'm looking for someone."

He waved an impatient hand towards the common room. "Go ahead."

"He's a minstrel named Gayland Bellmore."

"No one of that name's playing here." He turned to go.

"No! No, wait. Please," she added, as he looked at her irritably. "I thought...if he's played here in the past, maybe you know where he lives."

"My dear girl, musicians play here all the time. How in Freyn's name could I keep track of them, even if I wanted to? Anyway, they're a shiftless lot. Rarely stay long in one place." He waved a dismissive hand and hurried off. Cat stared after him, then left and trudged across the road to another inn.

At the seventh inn, she met with a kinder, if no more productive, response. The landlady, a round-faced, dimpled woman with kind eyes, thought for a moment before shaking her head. "Bellmore...Bellmore... No. I'm sorry, dear."

Cat swallowed her disappointment and smiled at the woman. "It's all right. Could you tell me how much a room costs for the night?" It was growing dark, and she was tired. Besides which, her stomach had been reminding her for the last hour that it needed feeding.

"Fifty coppers, plus another fifteen for supper and breakfast in the morning."

Cat gasped. "Oh." That was more than half the money she owned. She turned to go.

"Wait." The woman was looking at Cat, a frown puckering her forehead. "Do you have a place to stay tonight?"

"No, but –"

"Well, as it happens, we're short-handed tonight. Jena's laid up with a bad headache. If you don't mind scrubbing pots, you can have a bite to eat and a bed to sleep in. The bed's just a mat on the kitchen floor, mind."

"That will be fine." Cat followed the landlady into the kitchen.

The meal was filling, and Cat didn't mind scrubbing pots, but later, as she lay on her mat on the stone floor, she stared wide-eyed into the embers glowing in the fireplace and couldn't sleep.

Where was her father? How could she find him? He could be anywhere in this vast, indifferent city.

Was he even here? It was a month now since Master Weaver had cast his finding spell. What if Gayland had wandered off? Lianna had always said he grew restless if he stayed long in one place.

No. He must be here. She wouldn't believe otherwise. But how long would it take her to find him? How long would it take before her money ran out?

The embers had almost died by the time Cat fell into a fitful, restless sleep.


THE NEXT MORNING, after a filling breakfast of porridge, she set off on her rounds, tramping from inn to inn and – after telling herself sternly that she could and must do it – from tavern to tavern. The taverns weren't as bad as she'd feared, being quiet and almost deserted at this time of day. At noon, she spent a few of her precious coppers on a hot meat pie, bought from a stall in the street. It was no use asking questions at inns and taverns now: they were crowded with paying customers. She wandered about the streets, stopping at every second or third stall to gawk at brass pots, brightly coloured beads, pewter mugs, unfamiliar fruit; to finger embroidered cloth and supple leather; to sniff bundles of kala roots and packets of exotic spices. In the background, always, was the boom of the waterfall, drawing her eyes again and again to the shining tower of mist. Once a cart almost ran her down as she stood gazing at the falls. The driver cursed and spat.

Cat flushed and hurried away. It was time to resume her search anyway.

As the day wore on, her hunt took her away from the harbour area. Inns and taverns grew further apart. By late afternoon, her feet were sore from walking and her shoulders ached from carrying her pack.

At one tavern, she thought Freyn was finally smiling on her.

"Bellmore, Bellmore," the tavern owner said, turning the name over on his tongue. "Didn't we have a musician named Bellmore playing here a few weeks back?" he called to his wife, who stopped wiping tables and glanced up.

"A man in his early middle years, with longish yellow hair?"

"I...I think so," Cat said cautiously. For the first time, it occurred to her that she might not recognize her father if she saw him.

"A beautiful voice he had, and a lovely touch on the lute."

"That must be him," Cat said eagerly. "Where does he live?"

The woman shook her head. "I've no idea. And it's not likely he'll be back. He wanted more coins than we could give him. A few coppers are all we can afford, plus a meal and a drink, of course. He did have a beautiful voice," she said again.

With renewed hope, Cat plunged anew into her search. Perhaps he had sung at nearby taverns as well.

But all she met was indifferent shrugs, curt "nos," and regretful shakes of the head.

She emerged from one tavern into the gathering dusk and blinked back angry tears. They might be busy, but they needn't brush her aside like a bothersome fly. She wanted to kick the building behind her or break into a storm of tears.

She took deep breaths of the cool evening air, trying to regain her composure. If her feet didn't hurt so much... And she was hungry. At the last inn, she'd asked the price of a meal, but turned away upon hearing the answer. She wasn't going to spend fifteen of her meagre supply of coins on dinner.

But it wasn't her hunger, her fatigue, or her aching feet that made her feel like a grey rain cloud. It was the frustration, the futility of her quest.

There must be some other way of finding her father. Some better way.

She was too tired to think of one now. She needed food in her stomach and a bed to sleep in. She dragged herself back to the inn where she'd stayed the night before.

The landlady shook her head when Cat asked if she could work for her room and board again. "Jena's back. I'm sorry."

Something cold moved in Cat's stomach. It had been foolish to count on free lodging. But oh, to spend so many of her few coins on food and a bed for the night... And how long would it be before she found her father?

"Do you know of another inn that needs help?"

"I don't, but you can ask around."

"Thank you."

Cat turned to go, then stopped. The street outside was filled with shadows. She swallowed. Turned around.

"Could I sleep in the kitchen again? For free?"

Her grandmother would be horrified. Ashdales didn't ask for charity. But she was so tired. And the night was so dark.

The landlady hesitated. "You're new in Freyfall, aren't you?"

Cat nodded.

The woman sighed. "Very well. It's no time for a young girl to be roaming the streets. You can stay. But only for tonight, mind. And you'll have to pay for your food."

Cat smiled gratefully and headed for the kitchen.

Tomorrow, she promised herself. I'll think of a plan tomorrow.

## Street Life

**A**FINDING SPELL.

She awoke with the plan as clear in her head as though the night had printed it there.

Master Weaver had not been able to locate Gayland Bellmore beyond the general vicinity of Freyfall. But wouldn't a Freyfall wizard, familiar with the streets, be able to pinpoint his exact whereabouts? Also – disloyal though the thought might be – wouldn't a Freyfall wizard be more accomplished than one from small, isolated Frey-under-Hill?

There was only one problem. Finding spells cost money. Master Weaver had charged two silver coins, and she had less than one.

She must find work.

Filled with new energy, she bounced off her straw mat, splashed cold water on her face, then hurried to the common room for breakfast.

It was still early, and the room was almost deserted. The woman who plunked a bowl of oatmeal in front of her didn't look overly busy. Squinting at her in the sunlight pouring in through the east window, Cat asked, "Could you tell me who the best wizards in Freyfall are?"

"Wizards, is it? Well, I don't have much dealings with them myself, but I've heard of some. Konrad Spellman, for sure. His family's been wizards in Freyfall since Freyn knows when. You can't go wrong with him. Others... Let me see. There's a Master Clarke. I've heard he's good. And Master Wiseman. Or is it Wishman? Wish something or other. But the best wizards cost more money than the price of a bushel of herring," she added, with a glance at Cat's plain blue dress.

Would the spell cost more than two silver coins? For a moment, Cat's elation flickered. But surely she could earn two or three coins. Or even more.

"Can you tell me where I could find work?"

The woman pursed her lips. "Work's none too plentiful these days. Too many people moving here lately, especially those from the hills. Some say it's because they've been turned off their farms, but others claim it's because their farms aren't doing so well any more. Life's never been the same since the wizards sent some of our rain to Uglessia. Silly thing to do, if you ask me. Robbing us to help foreigners. And then they come here and take our jobs away from us. I've nothing against Uglessians, mind, strange looking though they be with their six fingers and all. But who comes first, them or us, that's what I'd like to know.

36

Strangest thing of all, though, is that some Freyans have married Uglessians, yes, and Islandians too. Like I said, I've nothing against them, but folk should stick to their own kind. I don't like these newfangled ways. Now, in my granny's day –"

Cat broke in, desperate to stem this torrent of words. "You don't know where I can find work, then?"

"Umm. Have you ever worked in a shop? Or looked after children? There's usually some rich folk wanting a nursemaid."

Cat shook her head.

"What about sewing? Dressmakers always need good fast sewers."

"I'm not very good at sewing," Cat confessed.

"What *have* you done?"

"I...I've helped my mother and grandmother in the house. And my grandfather on the farm."

"Well, farm labour's no use here. I suppose you might get work cleaning in a house or an inn. But like I say, jobs are hard to come by these days."

Cat winced, then straightened her shoulders. You can do it, she told herself fiercely. Don't give up before you even try. You can find a job.

"Thank you," she said.

The woman seemed inclined to linger. Cat was relieved when a newcomer demanded service. She finished her porridge quickly and emerged into the sun-filled street.

Stall owners were just beginning to draw up their shutters and put out their wares. Aside from them and a stray cat, the street was deserted. There was still a faint chill to the air. Cat shivered as she bent to stroke the cat, which gave her a disdainful look and stalked on.

Settling her pack comfortably on her shoulders, Cat set off for the inns she'd already visited, this time with a different question.

By midafternoon, the pack weighed heavily on her drooping shoulders. No one needed help; no one knew anyone else who needed help. Cat stood gazing at the carts and people passing by and wondered what to do. A faint headache nagged her. She rubbed her forehead. Tears pricked her eyes.

A thread of melody, gay, lilting, filtered through her misery. Glancing about, she spotted the source of the music. A flute player stood on a corner, surrounded by a small but growing audience. The tune he played reminded Cat of the clear brook that danced through the meadow at home. It drew her as honey draws bears.

She stood entranced as song followed song – laughing jigs, haunting laments, one that made Cat think of swallows' flight. Other people came and went. Some threw coins that landed like copper beads at the flutist's feet.

As the final tune died away, Cat felt someone brush past. Startled, she turned, but couldn't make out who it had been. Turning back, she watched the musician gather up the coins and stow them in his pockets. The audience dispersed. One man was unusually tall, with flaxen hair that flowed down his back to his waist. Cat stared. Was he a Uglessian? She'd never seen one, though she'd heard so much about them. She watched him until he disappeared around a corner.

The music had ended, the magic was gone. Sighing, Cat returned to her own concerns.

The most pressing one was hunger. Her stomach kept reminding her that it hadn't been fed since early morning, and the smell of frying sausage from a nearby stall made her mouth water. Much as she hated to do so, she must spend some of her few coppers on food. Reluctantly, she reached into her right pocket.

There was nothing there.

Cat frowned. Had she put her money in the other pocket? She'd thought... She reached in.

Nothing.

She'd had eighty-two coppers this morning. They couldn't be lost. Frantically, she dug into her pockets. Not a single coin met her groping fingers.

Was it possible she'd put the money in her pack and for-gotten she'd done so? Hands shaking, she removed the pack from her back and undid the straps.

Nothing.

Heedless of curious passersby, she knelt on the cobble-stones. One by one, she took each item of clothing out and shook it.

Nothing.

She checked her pockets again.

Nothing.

Cat knelt in the middle of her meagre possessions and stared ahead, unseeing. She couldn't have lost her money.

Had she left it at the inn this morning? No. She remembered fingering the coins as she walked down the street. Was that the last time she'd touched them? No. She had clutched them as she left the last inn, needing their solid reassurance.

Then where? When?

The brush against her arm.

Was that it? Had unknown fingers reached into her pocket, stolen her money?

What could she do? She had no idea who the thief was, where he had gone. She couldn't go to the authorities with no facts. They wouldn't help her.

No one would help her. She was in Freyfall with no family, no friends, no shelter, no food, and now no money.

Why had she come? Why had she left Frey-under-hill, left her mother, her grandparents, people she knew? To find her father? He didn't want her. He'd never wanted her. If he had, he wouldn't have left her.

Stupid. Stupid, stupid, stupid, stupid, *stupid.*

"What are you doing?"

The shrill voice broke into her fog of despair. She looked up – she didn't have to look far – into a round, rather grubby face topped by a mop of rusty-coloured curls.

"Nothing." She picked up her clothes and put them back in her pack.

"Why was your clothes on the ground? Is it a game?"

She wished the boy would go away. She grabbed her pack and rose. "I was looking for something."

"What?"

Cat hesitated. But the need to tell someone, even a small child, was pressing. "My money. I've lost it."

"Oh. Are you gonna sell your clothes to get some more? My mam did that once."

"Glynn!" A woman grabbed the boy's hand. "Stop dawdling. And don't pester people." She gave Cat an incurious glance as she dragged the boy away. He looked back over his shoulder and waved his free hand.

Sell her clothes. Maybe she should.

What did she have? A spare petticoat, spare underwear, one dress, one skirt, two blouses. That was all, except for the clothes she was wearing – and the tin whistle. And that she wouldn't sell.

Grim-faced, Cat set out to find a stall owner who wanted used clothes. At least she was no longer hungry. Her stomach was too tight. The smell of frying fish from the stall she passed made her feel sick.

BY NIGHTFALL, that was no longer true. Her stomach was uncomfortably empty and the smell of food made her head swim. But at least she had twenty-five coppers, clutched tightly in her hand. She could eat.

She'd hoped for more. All afternoon, she'd walked up and down the streets, inspecting clothing stalls, occasionally approaching possible buyers. Most, when learning she wanted to sell, not buy, had brushed her aside. Others glanced at her clothes, then shook their heads. Finally, she'd gone up to a stall just as its owner was rolling down the shutters. The counter was laden with trousers, skirts, shirts, cloaks, and shawls. Shabby clothes on a shabby stall in a shabby street.

"Please, will you buy these?" Desperately, she'd thrust the clothes in front of him.

He'd pawed through them. "Twenty-five coppers for the lot."

She swallowed. "They're worth more than that."

He shrugged. "Take it or leave it."

All day, she'd watched people barter. But she'd never bargained in her life. And it was getting dark. And she hadn't eaten since early morning. "All right."

At the next food stall, Cat bought a sausage in a bun and ate it greedily. She was still hungry when she finished, but she couldn't afford more. The sausage had cost seven coppers. Licking her fingers, she walked slowly on, wondering what to do. The street, so busy earlier, was now almost deserted. The stalls and buildings loomed, dark shadows lit only by the first faint stars of evening. The moon had not yet risen. A cool breeze sighed of lost times. Cat shivered, and wished she had a warmer cloak.

She needed to find shelter. But where? She had no money for a night's lodging. Unless...perhaps inns in this poorer part of town charged less. A lot less.

She had passed an inn a few blocks back. She retraced her steps, wishing her legs didn't ache so from all the walking. Her right foot was growing a huge blister.

The inn was small and noisy. Sounds of revelry came from the common room, where the customers seemed already well into their pints of ale. Cat had to wait several minutes before she was noticed.

"Yes?"

"How much is a room for the night?"

"Thirty-five coppers."

"Oh." Cat closed her eyes briefly, then opened them again. "Do you have any work I could do in exchange for a room?"

The landlord, a tall, burly man with a ship's prow of a nose, looked her up and down. Cat shrank from his gaze. "No." He turned to go.

"Wait," Cat called. He looked at her over his shoulder. She gulped. "Could I...do you have a place where I could sleep? Not a room, just a place to lie down. In the kitchen. Or the stable loft."

He spat. "I have no room for beggars. Join the others in the street."

Cat's face flamed. Hot tears sprang to her eyes. Hastily, she turned away to hide them. She fled.

A beggar. Was that what she was? She, an Ashdale of Ashdale Farm, where her family had lived good, honest, independent lives for generations? People at home might look down on her because she was the abandoned child of a wandering minstrel, but she had never been called a beggar before.

Join the others in the street, he had said. Where did they sleep, these others? On the cobblestones?

She couldn't keep on walking. Her foot hurt too much, and the shadows were too dense, too threatening. The wind had picked up. It blew a piece of paper in front of her. Cat jumped.

Finally, she found a deeply recessed doorway in a darkened building and sat down, leaning wearily against the wooden wall. She stared up at the sky, where a silvery quarter moon now hung, and remembered other nights, when she had taken her blankets to the hilltop above the house and lain looking up at the stars. Sometimes her mother would lie beside her and point out the three stars that made up the mouse's tail. She had been a child then, and had thought the mouse looked very real. She had giggled with delighted terror when the moon sailed too close to the mouse's open mouth. She remembered one sultry night, when her grandparents had joined them on the grass, and the four of them had gazed up at the sky together.

She tried to stop them, but the tears came, flooding her eyes and running down her cheeks. She slipped to the ground and huddled in her cloak, shaking with sobs.

## MAB

EIGHTEEEN COINS DIDN'T LAST VERY LONG. Three days later, still hungry and light-headed after eating a bun – the only food she'd had all day – Cat stared at the one coin left her and felt panic flow closer, threatening to drown her.

She had tramped the streets the last three days – limped them, actually – looking for work. She had tried inns and private homes and even taverns. She had crossed bridges to the west and east banks of the city. Everyone had all the help they needed; no one wanted her.

*Someone must. I just have to keep looking.*

Yes. But in the meantime, what did she do? Starve? Beg? In the past days, she had noticed thin waifs in rags, bent old women, crippled men, holding out pleading hands. But even if everything in her hadn't flinched away from the thought, she doubted her success as a beggar. She wasn't crippled or ragged or thin – not yet, anyway.

It started to rain, a fine, drizzling rain that threatened to go on and on. Cat looked up at the grey, overhanging sky. Still several hours of daylight, she judged, or what passed for daylight on this gloomy day. Several hours before the shops closed. Cat had learned that shop owners did not welcome people who took refuge in their doorways. Not if those people were poor. No one welcomed you if you were poor, not even in this scruffy neighbourhood. Cat shivered and wrapped her cloak tighter around herself.

She must find shelter. Wandering away from the main streets, she soon found herself walking down a road lined with small, dilapidated houses. They looked as depressed as she was, their roofs sagging as dismally as her rain-drenched hair. She was cold, and wet, and hungry.

*Creak.*

Cat looked toward the sound. Her eyes sharpened as she examined the small lean-to where a door swung drunkenly. Could she stay there? Her eyes moved to the house beside it. It seemed empty, perhaps deserted.

The lean-to was dark, with a dank, musty smell. She stopped in the doorway to let her eyes adjust, then moved cautiously inside.

Something rustled in the corner.

Cat froze.

"Who be there?" The voice was indistinct, muffled.

Cat was still.

She heard the sound of a flint being struck, then blinked as the wavering light of a candle lit the shed.

"Oh, it be a girl. Come in, child. There be room for two,

and I don't bite. Though I'm tempted, sometimes, I be that hungry." A small gurgle of laughter followed.

Cat swallowed. The candle created caverns of black hollows in the seamed, toothless face she saw before her, a face topped by sparse white hair. But the voice was kind. She took a step forward.

"The ground be damp. Come share me shawl."

Cat made out the dim outline of the shawl the old woman sat on. After a moment, she said, "Thank you," and seated herself on its far edge.

"Best not waste me candle." The woman blew it out. In the darkness, Cat was very aware of her companion's breath, whistling in and out, and of the smell of old, unwashed flesh. She breathed through her mouth.

They sat in silence for a while, listening to the drip of the rain. Gradually, Cat warmed up. Her shivering stopped. Her eyes closed.

"Be you hungry, child?"

Cat's eyes flew open. "What?"

"Be you hungry?"

Cat's stomach rumbled at the very thought of food. The old woman chuckled and put a piece of hard bread in Cat's hand. Cat's stomach rumbled again. She raised the bread to her mouth.

Then she paused. Slowly, she lowered her hand. "Are you sure? I mean...do you have enough for yourself?"

"Bless you, don't you worry about me. I get enough to get me by."

Cat took a bite. "How?" she asked, chewing the dry,

hard bread. "How do you get by?"

"I have me ways. Folks be kind enough to give me a coin or two, times. Then I take it to the bakers and ask for their stale bread, what they'd throw away, else. Don't cost more than a copper, and sometimes they give it to me when I has no coins. Harder to eat than it used to be, mind, with me teeth gone, but I manage. Sometimes I gets bones from the butchers, too."

"Oh," Cat said slowly.

"You be new here, then?"

"Yes."

"Come looking for work, I suppose, like so many folk. Be you from the hills?"

"No."

"From a farm that's not doing so well, then. Many be too dry, these days."

"So I heard. Someone told me there's not been enough rain in Freya ever since the wizards sent some of our rain to Uglessia."

The woman snorted. "That be foolishness. I'se lived long enough to know we had plenty of bad times before ever the wizards shifted the winds. This last bad time's only been three years, whiles the rain's been shifted for forty." She snorted again.

"Oh." Cat absorbed this, then said, "Actually, I didn't come here looking for work; I came to find my father." She heard her own words with surprise. She rarely shared confidences. Why tell a stranger her story? But the darkness was friendly, and there was something about this old woman...

She hesitated only briefly, then plunged on.

When she had finished, there was a thoughtful silence. Then the woman said, "Your da be a musician then, be he?"

"Yes."

"He'll be here for the council, then."

"What council?"

"The wizards' council. Wizards from the three lands be coming here."

"Master Weaver – the wizard at home – mentioned it. But what –"

"There's to be music for the queen and all them great wizards, when Queen Elira opens the council on Midsummer Night, and a contest to choose who's to sing, judged by the queen's own musicians. Many's the musician will be trying for that, I be thinking."

So that was why Gayland was in Freyfall. And he'd be here till after the musical trials. Till after the council, in fact: he'd be sure to be chosen. Oh, to be there when he played for Queen Elira and the wizards!

"Thank you," she said softly.

"Nothing to thank me for, but you be welcome, child."

"Cat. My name's Cat."

A wheezing laugh came from the darkness. "Glad there be a cat here to keep away the rats."

"Rats?" Cat shuddered.

"Nay, there may be none here. But if there be, no need for *you* to fear them, I be thinking." Another wheezing laugh. "I be Mab," the old woman added. "And it be time for us folk to go to sleep."

Cat smiled into the darkness. "Good night, Mab." She took off her cloak, folded it over a couple of times to make a pillow, then settled down on the rest of it and her share of the shawl. A moment later, despite the chill dampness, despite her fear of rats, she was asleep.

SHE WOKE feeling as full of possibilities as the morning itself. After breakfast – more stale bread – she and Mab emerged into the puddly, sun-bright street.

"I be on me way, then," Mab said.

Impulsively, Cat leaned down to kiss the wrinkled cheek. She had to lean a long way. Last night, she hadn't realized how small Mab was.

The old woman touched Cat's face lightly. "Freyn smile on you, child."

"And on you."

Cat watched Mab walk away, her steps surprisingly sure on the slippery cobblestones. For a moment, she wanted to run after her, stay with her. But Mab would do better on her own. And Cat had things to do. She would find work. She would find her father.

Cat walked back to the busier commercial streets.

Nothing had changed, really, except that she had learned that one copper would buy a loaf of stale bread and that Gayland would stay in Freyfall at least until after the contest. But everything seemed different, as though Mab's kindness had transformed the world. Cat raised her eyes to the sun-kissed mist of the waterfall and realized, with mild surprise, that she hadn't looked at it for the last three days.

As though echoing her mood, the gay notes of a song met her as she rounded a corner. Cat smiled and stopped. A woman with bright copper hair sang to a tune a man played on his tin whistle. Passersby paused to listen. Some threw coins into the man's hat.

The woman's voice was pleasant but a bit thin. I could do better, thought Cat.

Her eyes widened.

She could do better. She could sing. She could play her father's tin whistle. She could have coins flung her way.

Could she? She had never sung in public except at her mother's wedding. Would she dare stand on a street corner and sing?

What if no one stopped to listen? What if people jeered?

If she didn't dare, what then? She needed money to eat. She needed money to give to a wizard to locate her father. And she had discovered, these last four days, that finding work here was as hopeless as catching fish in a nearly dry stream.

Cat took a deep breath, then let it out slowly.

Turning away from the musicians, she walked slowly up the street. She must find her own corner, one that was busy but not too noisy. She passed several possible sites before she forced herself to stop. Taking off her cloak, she spread it on the cobblestones at her feet. Despite the brightness of the day, there was a cool bite to the wind. She shivered.

Her voice wasn't strong enough to attract an audience. She took out her whistle and blew a tentative note. Then, a trifle shakily, she began to play.

The first tune led to another, and another, and another. People spared her only passing glances as they hurried by. One woman paused for a moment, then walked on.

Would no one stop? Cat was beginning to despair when a small boy with curly reddish-brown hair dragged his mother to a standstill in front of her. It was the same boy who'd spoken to her the day her money was stolen. A lucky or an unlucky omen?

Cat finished the tune and put her whistle away, her fingers shaking, and launched into a song. It was one she had learned as a child, about a dog chasing his tail, and it soon had the boy giggling. His mother, looking impatient but resigned, stayed. A third person joined the small audience.

Cat sang a song she had heard the rowers chant, then a traditional tune used when herding cows to pasture. She followed these with a love ballad and a mother's lament for a lost child. She sang till she had almost exhausted her repertoire, till her voice was hoarse.

Some of her listeners stayed only briefly, for one song or part of one. The small boy – Glynn, wasn't it? – had to be dragged away. Cat was sorry to see him go.

When she finished, the sun was high in the sky and her stomach demanded attention. There was a bright spattering of copper coins on her cloak.

Seven. Seven copper coins. Not much for a morning's work, but enough. Resolutely, Cat ignored the smell of hot beef pies and headed for a bakeshop and the promise of cheap stale bread. She would have to sleep in a doorway or a deserted shed again tonight.

But seven coins were enough. Enough to buy food. Enough to give her hope.

# Going to the Wizard

CAT STUDIED HER AUDIENCE. AFTER TEN days of street singing, she was becoming more adept at guessing what songs her listeners would appreciate and how much they might give.

This was her third day at this particular location, on a corner of a broad boulevard on the east bank. The pace was slightly less hectic here than elsewhere, the people more prosperous. It was a good spot.

She saw a couple of children. Good. Children were usually easy to please, and their parents grateful. There was a matronly woman with a large shopping basket. She might not stay long. Two elderly men looked like stayers, but they also looked too threadbare to throw many coins. Cat's eyes lingered on a tall, pale young woman whose waist-length hair was the colour of rich cream. A Uglessian, surely. Cat wondered what she would think of her music.

Her eyes scanned the assembly again, hoping to see the dark-haired boy who'd come partway through her first performance on this corner, and returned again yesterday. He wasn't there. She shouldn't feel so disappointed. But he had listened so intently. *And* given generously.

A heavy cart rumbled by. She waited till it passed, then began her next song. Just as she finished, the boy slipped in at the back of the group. She smiled.

"My next piece will be 'The Islands,'" she announced. It was one of her favourites, but difficult to sing, especially without accompaniment. Somehow, the boy's presence gave her confidence.

The song told the story of wizards who, forty years earlier, had braved the fog and rocks that lay in the seas around Islandia to learn the secrets of the Wise Women's magic. She sang the opening bars then almost stopped, astounded. A lute had added its melody to hers.

The dark-haired boy was playing it, and playing it beautifully. After a fractional pause, Cat continued. Together, lute and voice conveyed the dangers of the voyage and the clash of people and ideas, then the joyful conclusion as a Wise Woman of Islandia married a Freyan wizard and love conquered all.

A burst of applause greeted the final notes. Cheeks flushed, Cat gazed around the much augmented audience and smiled shyly.

"Sing 'The Rains of Uglessia,'" someone called. Cat glanced at the boy. He nodded. They swung into the story of young Kerstin Speller, who had journeyed to Uglessia, the land of Freya's enemies, and how she had fought to bring peace to the two nations. Cat sang the final line, "The rains came/the rivers ran/the land grew green." When she ended, the lute continued for a minute and Cat heard, like an echo of her words, the patter of rain, the rush of water. Then the lute quieted too. There was a moment of hushed silence, followed by rapturous applause. Cat's eyes shone.

As the clapping faded away, Cat heard a man mutter, "It's all well and good in a song, but they should never have given away our rain." His companion nudged him, but the Uglessian woman's head had already jerked his way. She stared at him for a moment, then turned and left.

Cat was sorry, but had no time to think about it. People were calling out requests.

Time flowed by, carried on a wave of song. Her singing seemed effortless, supported and lifted by the lute. She stopped only when her voice cracked.

A tall man in a black cloak, who'd been there for most of the performance, laughed. "The wages of too much singing," he said, and tossed a coin. Others followed his example. The crowd dispersed.

Cat stared at the money on her cloak. Was that...? She fell to her knees. Yes! Silver gleamed among the copper. One silver and – she counted quickly – sixty, no, sixty-two copper coins. Add them to the fifty-eight she had managed to save and she had enough. She could afford a finding spell.

"You sing beautifully," said a light tenor voice.

Startled, Cat glanced up, then scrambled to her feet. She had forgotten the lute player.

"Thank you," she stammered. "You do too. I mean, play beautifully." He should get half the earnings: without him, she wouldn't have nearly so much. But oh, to give up her dream... Never mind. She wasn't giving it up, only postponing it.

She held out her hands. "Here. Half of this is yours."

He drew back. "I don't want it. That's not why I played."

She looked at him more closely, noticing the fine material of his well-cut clothes, the polished wood of his lute. He was about her own age, she judged, with a thin triangular face and sharp, pointed features. His eyes were dark, almost black, as was the hair that fell forward onto his forehead.

"But you deserve it," she insisted.

"I don't want it. It's yours."

A minute ago, the thought of giving up some of her money had hurt like a cut finger. Now she flushed with sudden resentment, very conscious of her soiled dress and uncombed hair.

"Maybe we could perform together again," the boy said eagerly. "Do you come here every day? I could come...well, not all the time, but this week anyway. We make a good team," he added, and smiled. The smile transformed his face, warmed it, softened it, made him...vulnerable, Cat thought.

She shook her head. "No. This is the last time I'll be here."

"You'll sing somewhere else, you mean? I could meet –"

"No. I won't be singing at all after today. I have all the money I need."

"But... Don't you like it?"

Like performing on street corners? Like singing for money? She opened her mouth to give a scathing reply, then closed it.

She *did* like it. Despite her shaking hands, her dry mouth, her fear that no one would listen, no one throw the coins she needed so desperately, she *did* enjoy it.

She didn't say this, though, just thrust the coins into her pockets.

Without a word, he turned and walked away.

Cat watched him go. She hesitated. She could run after him, ask him his name. Perhaps after she'd found her father, the three of them could play and sing together – her father, this boy, and herself. But he was already halfway down the street, taking giant strides. And she had other things to do.

Lunch first. Then the wizard.

LOCATING MASTER SPELLMAN'S HOUSE was easy. Everyone knew the whereabouts of the best wizard in Freyfall. He lived at 6 Gotham Street, not far from where Cat had been that morning.

As she got nearer and nearer, Cat's steps grew slower and slower. The houses on either side of her were tall, imposing buildings with bow windows and elegant stone facades. Maybe she should find a public fountain, wash her face and hands at least. She couldn't do much about the rest. She probably smelled.

But there was no fountain in sight. Besides... Cat

winced. Three days ago, she'd tried to clean her face in one. A man had shouted at her, and she'd fled.

No. The wizard would have to take her the way she was.

There was nothing to distinguish number 6 from its neighbours except a small, discreet gold plaque on the green door saying simply, "Konrad Spellman, Wizard." Its very plainness was intimidating. Cat took several deep breaths, then tapped lightly.

After a moment, the door was opened by a tall, middle-aged woman whose hair was drawn back in a severe bun. She took one look at Cat and said, "Back door."

"I –"

"Those asking for work or charity go to the back door."

Two weeks ago, Cat would have been furious. Or ashamed. But two weeks of being told to go to the back or having doors slammed in her face had hardened her. She stuck her foot in the opening and said, "I want to see Master Spellman."

"I doubt Master Spellman wants to see you. Anyway –"

"I have money," Cat said quickly.

The woman sniffed. "Stolen probably."

This was too much. "It is not!"

Another woman appeared in the hall, a younger, shorter woman whose smooth brown hair was drawn up in a braid on top of her head. Worry lines were etched in her forehead. "Is something wrong, Mistress Fairway?"

"Just a ragamuffin at the door, Mistress Spellman."

Mistress Spellman? Cat took a closer look, and noticed the subtle elegance of the high-necked, dove-coloured dress, the lace at wrists and down the line of pearl buttons that decorated the bodice.

The younger woman smiled kindly at Cat. "Would you like some food? I think Cook has some leftover soup."

"I want to see the wizard. On business," Cat said tightly.

The woman's smile faded. "Oh dear."

"I have money," Cat repeated.

"It's not that. But I'm afraid my father-in-law is away. He won't be back for a week."

Cat felt as though a sharp pin had punctured her and let out all the breath inside.

There were other wizards.

But Konrad Spellman was the best. And she had hoped for this moment so long, worked for it...

Mistress Spellman must have seen Cat's dismay in her face. "Would you like to see my son? He's serving as an apprentice to my father-in-law."

Would an apprentice be able to find Gayland Bellmore? Well, she could ask. Surely he would tell her if he couldn't. Cat nodded.

With a sniff, the housekeeper stepped aside.

"This way." Mistress Spellman led Cat down a polished, richly tapestried hall. Cat glanced guiltily at her shoes and wondered whether the floor would have to be washed as soon as she left. She wiped her hands on her dress.

As they approached the rear of the house, her ears pricked up. Someone was playing a lute, quietly and expertly.

"Oh dear," Mistress Spellman murmured.

She tapped gently on a heavy oak door. The music died.

The woman opened the door. "Garth, there's someone here who requires your services."

Cat gasped. Over Mistress Spellman's shoulder, she saw a boy rising quickly from a stool, lute in hand, a flush staining his thin face. She had seen him before. That very morning. With the same lute.

# CAT

A WAVE OF COLOUR WASHED OVER THE BOY'S face at the sight of Cat. His mother looked at him, then at Cat, and repeated, "There's someone here who requires your services."

"My services?" he asked after a moment.

"She came asking for your grandfather. Since he's away, I thought you might be able to help her."

"Yes. Yes, of course." He fumbled with the lute, then placed it on the stool.

"Garth..." Mistress Spellman looked at it reproachfully.

"Yes, I know," he said shortly.

His mother sighed, then smiled at Cat. "After you've finished your business here, come to the kitchen for a meal. Garth will show you the way."

"Thank you," Cat mumbled, though, in truth, she had no intention of staying in the house one minute more than she needed to. This room made her feel even poorer and dirtier than the hall had. She glanced at the book-lined shelves, the oak table, the tall windows richly draped in crimson, the soft rug beneath her feet. No wonder this boy – Garth Spellman, he must be called – had declined his share of the money they'd earned.

Mistress Spellman left.

"What do you want?" Garth asked. "Sit down. Please," he added, gesturing jerkily to a chair beside her. He hadn't looked at her since his first startled glance.

Cat sat tentatively on the edge of a high-backed wooden chair with intricately carved arms. Across from her, a mirror with an ornate gilded frame hung on the wall. It showed her a girl whose plain blue dress was torn and smudged with dirt, whose heavy tawny hair hung in matted locks around a face that was tired and thinner than the one she knew. And dirtier. She averted her eyes.

"I want a finding spell," she announced.

"Simple or complex?"

She had no idea. Master Weaver had not asked this question. "A two-coin one," she said firmly.

"A two –" The boy was looking at her now, his mouth agape, his eyes frankly astonished.

Cat swallowed. Were her two silver coins not enough? "That's what the wizard at home charged."

"I see."

It was obvious he didn't think it was adequate. "But if that's not enough here, I'll go," she said haughtily, if a trifle unsteadily, and rose. Her eyes fell on the lute and she added, even more haughtily, "More than a third of what I own belongs to you, anyway."

Garth made an impatient gesture. "I told you... Anyway, I didn't mean... Two coins are fine."

She looked at him doubtfully.

"Sit back down and tell me what you want." Garth sat down on the stool, carefully removing the lute first.

Cat reseated herself, still hesitant.

"Well?"

"I want you to find my father."

"Your father?" A gleam of amusement glinted in his eyes. "Is he lost, strayed, or stolen? I'm sorry," he said hastily as Cat flushed. "That was... I'm sorry. Tell me about him."

"His name is Gayland Bellmore, and he's somewhere in Freyfall, Master Weaver said."

"How did he know? Did he see a familiar landmark, or the name of a street, or –"

"He heard the waterfall."

"Oh. That doesn't help much. He could be anywhere in the city."

"That's why I'm here. I thought if a wizard from Freyfall saw him, he'd recognize the street."

"Perhaps."

Cat ignored the doubt in his voice. She dug in her pocket. "Here." Rising, she handed him the tin whistle. "This belonged to him."

Garth surveyed the whistle with interest. "Is he a musician too, then?"

"Yes," Cat said proudly. "A good one."

"Hmm." Garth fingered the whistle. "What... Never mind." He gave himself a small shake and asked briskly,

"When did he last hold this?"

"Twelve years ago."

*What?*" Garth stared at her, his mouth agape again. "You expect me to find a man using a whistle he hasn't touched for twelve years?"

She returned his stare. "Master Weaver did."

He shook his head, in wonder, not disbelief. "He must be a very good wizard indeed, this Master Weaver of yours."

"I...I suppose he is. He was taught by Morgan Speller."

"By Morgan Speller?" Garth sounded impressed. "He was one of the best wizards in Freya."

Cat swallowed. "Do you mean you can't find Father, even though Master Weaver did?"

Garth flushed. "You don't know what you're asking. To expect me to find a man I've never met, using only a whistle he hasn't touched in twelve years, one you've probably handled since then, masking all traces of him... You don't know much about magic, do you?"

"If I did, I'd find Father myself rather than come to you." Her eyes stung with angry, frustrated tears.

"Well, I can't help you," he said flatly. "If Grandfather were here... But he's not."

She stood up, legs trembling. "I'll go to another wizard, then."

"Yes, do that." He held the whistle out to her. Wordlessly, she accepted it and walked towards the door.

"Wait," he called just as she reached it. She turned.

He was frowning. "Look," he began, then paused, gnawing at his lower lip. "Your money... Some wizards might not think it's enough."

"You said –"

"Two coins are fine for me, but then I'm only an apprentice. Here."

Cat stared at the outstretched hand, then at Garth's face. Eight silver coins, to add to her two. Ten coins. Was that what most wizards charged? Was that what he should have charged? Was that what Master Weaver would have asked for if he hadn't known her, if he hadn't been kind?

This boy was being kind too. His kindness stung. She shook her head fiercely.

"You can consider it a loan if you like. Pay me back when you've found your father."

For a moment she wavered. Then she remembered Master Weaver's vision of Gayland sitting in a small, shabby room. Her father might not have eight coins to spare. She would not go to him owing money. She shook her head again.

Garth bit his lip. "Maybe... Look, I don't know whether I can help. I...well, I'm not even a very good apprentice. Grandfather says I let my mind wander too much, and I guess he's right. But maybe... Why don't you tell me more about your father? If I knew more, then just possibly..."

Was this charity too? Worse, was it a waste of her time and money? But the faint hope he held out to her was the only hope she had. She returned to the chair.

"What does your father look like?"

"He...I haven't seen him since I was three, but I think he's tall – medium tall, anyway. I know he has yellow hair."

Garth waited, but she said no more. He sighed.

"Does he look like you?"

"I...I think so. Mother sometimes said I reminded her of him."

"You said he's a musician. What does he play?"

"Everything. At least – He used this whistle, of course. And he plays the flute and a lute. He goes from place to place, playing the lute and singing. He has a beautiful voice."

"He's a wandering minstrel, then."

Cat stiffened. How often had she heard her father described this way, and always with a note of scorn? But the apprentice needed information. She nodded.

"What a wonderful life it must be." There was naked longing in his voice. Cat blinked.

"I think he's in Freyfall for the wizards' council," she volunteered. "Mab – an old woman I met – said musicians were to sing at it."

Garth nodded. "Yes, at the opening on Midsummer Night. Grandfather and his friends have been talking about the council for months. So have all the musicians in town. But...does your father write music, as well as play it? The contest rules say the songs must be sung by the composers, and must be about the three lands of Freya, Uglessia, and Islandia."

"Oh yes, he makes up songs," Cat said confidently. One of her few clear memories of Gayland was of him singing a laughing, bubbling song about Cat as a baby. Lianna still sang it, sometimes.

Garth frowned. "Have you thought of looking for him in the places musicians might go? They frequently play at inns and taverns."

"Yes. Oh yes, I've looked there. I've looked, and looked." Suddenly it all came tumbling out, her fruitless search, the shrugs, curt rebuffs, and shakes of the head that had met her question. Everything came out, in a jumbled rush, like objects falling from an upturned bag: the theft of her money, her visit to Master Weaver, her futile quest for work, her voyage to Freyfall, her hunger, the encounter with Mab, the days of roaming the city and singing on street corners. Everything except the reason behind it all: her mother's marriage to Kenton Herd. That was private.

When all the words had spilled out, Cat leaned back in her chair, feeling tired but surprisingly light. Garth had listened quietly, with only an occasional murmur of sympathy. Now he sighed.

"I can see why you want a finding spell. Well...I can't promise anything, mind you, but if you'll give me the whistle again, I'll try."

She handed it to him and watched intently as he bent over the instrument. His fingers ran over it, caressed it. He half raised it to his lips, then lowered it hastily and spoke the words of the spell. As she had done in Master Weaver's chamber, Cat could almost, but not quite, understand all the words, as though their meaning hung in the air just out of reach.

Her muscles tensed as she waited, her eyes fixed on Garth, whose own eyes had gone slightly out of focus as he gazed at the whistle. His frown deepened. Time seemed to slow, the air to go still, as minutes – or was it hours? – went by.

Then the frown disappeared, to be replaced by a look of dreamy absorption. Garth murmured a few words, so quietly that Cat couldn't catch them.

Something seemed to be happening to the room. Or was it to her? She felt dizzy. Sick. As though she were falling. As though...

The room wavered. Blurred.

Then it steadied, sharpened. But now it was larger, brighter, different. Birdsong filtered in through the closed window. The muted tread of feet in the hall was suddenly loud. And there were smells, new, tantalizing smells.

Cat blinked and shook her head, disturbed, then shook it again, even more alarmed by the strange feel of her neck muscles, the strange lack of the swing of heavy hair. She blinked once more. Looked around. Her eyes stopped on Garth's face.

He was staring at her. His eyes were huge, his mouth an open circle, his face the colour of muddy snow.

Cat stared back. Something was wrong. What...?

Slowly, reluctantly, as though pulled by strings, her gaze shifted. It moved to the mirror opposite her. Stopped.

She wasn't there. There was no fifteen-year-old girl with thick, matted hair and a dirty, ragged blue dress and grey cloak sitting on the high-backed chair. The dress and cloak were there, crumpled limply on the seat. But she, Cat, had disappeared.

In her place, crouched on the chair, hair on end, was a small, tawny cat.

# IN THE WIZARD'S HOUSE

SHE WAS A CAT.

She couldn't be. It was impossible.

But she was.

The mirror only confirmed it. Her body knew: the feel of alien muscles, the sights, sounds, and smells pouring in through feline senses.

Tremors shook her.

Run! screamed a voice inside her. Spring to the floor. Run howling from this room, from this house. Run. Run. But where?

Calm. She must be calm. She was still herself. Still Cat. She *was.* She must believe that.

It was the spell, the spell the boy had cast. It must be.

If he could turn her into a cat, then he could turn her back into a girl.

She stared at him.

Garth's face was bone-white now, his eyes still wide

with shock. The hand he held to his mouth shook.

"I...I'm sorry," he stammered. "I didn't mean...I don't know how..."

His voice echoed in the still room. Almost still room. Behind the wall, something scratched. A mouse? Cat's ears pricked.

Garth swallowed. "I don't...I don't know how I did it," he repeated. "I made the spell right. I'm sure I did. It's not...I've done it before. Then I was looking at the whistle. I was concentrating, I really was, though its music kept calling to me... But I was concentrating. For a moment, I almost saw... But pictures of you kept slipping in, because you'd had the whistle so long. I saw you playing it in a pasture, surrounded by cows, and sitting on a mossy rock by a stream. The tune sounded like water running over stones, like the stream itself."

The dreamy look reappeared on his face. Then it vanished. "I repeated the spell. At least, I thought I did. I must...I must have said the wrong words."

Cat's claws dug into the chair. Wrong! Then make them right! Turn me back! She wanted to scream, but all that emerged was a loud meow.

"I can't," Garth said, as though he'd heard her unspoken cry. "If I knew what I'd said, I could reverse it. But I don't. I don't even know how to transform someone. Only the most powerful wizards do. I don't see how...I do know how to make an illusion. Maybe you just look like a cat." He brightened. "Do you still feel like a girl?"

Reluctantly, Cat shook her head.

He sighed. "I didn't think I'd done that. Still, if I reverse an illusion spell, maybe..." He paused, closed his eyes, then uttered words, clearly and with all the determination he would have used to push a large boulder uphill.

Nothing happened.

Garth's shoulders slumped. Watching him, Cat couldn't feel angry. She wished she could. Anger might warm the cold fear that twisted her entrails and sent shudders running through her body. She crouched lower in the chair.

"I guess I must have stumbled on the transformation spell by mistake, though I thought, I really thought, I was repeating the right words. If only I knew the transformation spell." He put his hands over his face, rubbed his eyes with the heels of his hands. Then he lowered them. "Grandfather's book!"

He strode over to the bookshelf. Cat's heart quickened. She watched intently as he examined the books, then took one down. It was thinner than most, and plainer, with no title etched onto its black binding.

"I think this might have it. The book's rare, and Grandfather never lets me touch it." He placed it on the desk and sat. With a trembling hand, he reached to open it.

There was a knock on the door.

Garth froze. Then, after one frantic glance around, he threw a handful of loose papers on top of the book and dashed over to Cat's chair. Snatching up her cloak and dress, he hid them behind his back.

"Come in."

The door opened and Mistress Fairway stepped inside. "Afternoon tea is served, Master Garth." Her eyes swept the room. "I see that – girl – is gone." Her gaze rested on Cat. "Where did that creature come from?"

"I...it jumped in through the window."

Mistress Fairway's eyes moved to the window.

"I'd opened it. Then I closed it. After the cat jumped in," Garth said hastily.

"Then I'll put it out again."

"No! No, please don't. I...I think it's hungry."

The housekeeper sniffed. "We can't feed all the stray cats in Freyfall."

"No, but...can't we keep this one? At least until after it's fed? Please."

Mistress Fairway hesitated, then shrugged. "It's not my place to decide who's to be let in, that's clear. While Master Spellman is away, your mother decides." She sounded as grim as if a naughty child had been left in charge. "In the meantime, your tea is waiting."

"I'll be there in a few minutes."

"Your tea is ready now." The woman's voice was glacial.

Garth backed up, hands still behind him, until he was behind the desk. Watching him, Cat knew he must be dropping her clothes to the floor and kicking them under the desk. In other circumstances, it would have been funny. She wished she found it funny now.

"I have to go," he told her apologetically. "I'll be back soon."

"Aren't you going to feed it?"

"What?"

"I thought you wanted to feed the creature."

"Oh. Yes, of course." Garth turned to Cat and waited.

She should jump down and follow him. She crept to the edge of the chair and peered down. The floor was a long way away. She shrank back.

Garth bent and lifted her. Cat stiffened, then forced herself to relax. Since she was too scared to jump, she'd have to let herself be carried.

Garth followed the housekeeper down the hall to a large room dominated by a massive dark table. Two places were set at the far end. Mistress Spellman was already seated at one. Her eyes lit up at the sight of Cat.

"A cat. What a beauty." She rose, came over to where Garth stood, and stroked Cat with gentle, loving fingers. A soft rumble emerged from Cat's throat. After a moment, she realized she was purring.

"Where did she come from?"

"Jumped in through the window," Garth mumbled.

"Master Garth thought we should feed it before sending it away," Mistress Fairway said from the doorway.

"Of course we shall. She must be hungry, poor love. Garth, what about the girl who was here earlier? I hope you gave her something to eat before she left."

Garth's face flamed. "No. She left in a hurry." He bent to place Cat on the floor.

"You surely don't mean to feed that cat in here," Mistress Fairway said sharply.

"I thought...I can give her scraps from my plate."

"The dining room is no place for a cat. If it must be fed, it can go to the kitchen."

"Perhaps that would be best, dear," Mistress Spellman said gently.

Garth's hold on Cat tightened. "All right. Sorry," he whispered in Cat's ear.

The kitchen was a big, well-scrubbed room lit by a square pane of glass and warmed by a large fireplace and wood stove. A plump, rosy-cheeked woman in a starched white apron stood over the stove, stirring a pot. Cat sniffed hungrily. Fish stew. A young serving girl was arranging pastries on a tray.

"Mistress Grove, may I have some food for this cat?"

"A cat, is it? A stray, I suppose, and hungry. Of course you may. Here, I'll get a saucer of milk. And maybe it would like some fish, too."

Cat ate the fish in three hungry gulps before turning her attention to the milk. She paused, not sure how to tackle it. But she had seen cats at home. She stuck out her tongue and placed it on the milk. After a couple of tries, the milk went down easily.

Garth knelt beside her. "I'll be back as soon as I can," he whispered, then rose and hurried out. Cat stopped lapping to watch him go. For a moment, she felt bereft, almost panicky. It was as though her last link to her true self was deserting her. Then she returned to the milk. He'd be back. And she was still hungry. She had days of deprivation to make up for.

The cook and the serving girl – Ellen, Mistress Grove called her – ignored Cat as they went about their work and filled the room with friendly chatter. Milk gone, Cat watched them for a while, then, instinctively, started to clean herself.

It was so easy. Far easier, Cat thought as she licked her paw then rubbed it across her face, than cleaning herself as a girl. Especially a girl on the streets.

Garth returned. He looked relieved when he saw Cat, as though afraid she might have disappeared during his absence. He bent to pick her up, but she meowed and stepped back. She would walk by herself.

"All right," Garth said quickly. "Follow me to the study."

Cat walked behind him, listening to the faint pad of her paws on the hall floor. How strange to have paws. And how strange to walk on four legs. What order did they go in?

Suddenly, what had been natural became confusing. Her legs tangled and collapsed under her.

Garth had reached the study door. He turned and saw her. Alarm sprang into his face. "What's wrong?"

Cat struggled to her feet. Don't think, she told herself. Just walk. But her mind wouldn't be still. She collapsed again.

Garth was beside her in an instant, picking her up. "Don't worry. You'll be yourself again soon." His words were more reassuring than his voice, which was shaking.

Mistress Fairway appeared in the hall. "I trust you're on your way to put that creature out."

"No. Not yet. Mother said I could keep her for a while," Garth added hastily as Mistress Fairway raised her eyebrows.

"A short while, I presume. I doubt Master Spellman would be happy to see a cat in his house upon his return." The housekeeper stalked away, her back stiff.

"A short while," Garth said, but he said it to Cat, not the

woman. He opened the study door and closed it behind him with a sigh of relief. "A very short while, cat." He laughed shakily. "When you're a girl again, I can find out what your name is, instead of just calling you cat. I was wondering what it was when I was working on the finding spell. On what was supposed to be the finding spell," he corrected himself. Setting Cat down, he went over to the desk, sat down, and removed the papers that hid the black book.

Cat forgot to breathe.

Garth drew the book towards him. He moved to open it.

He frowned. The book remained closed. His frown deepened. He took the book between both hands and tried again. Nothing happened. He spoke some words. Waited. Nothing.

Garth stayed still for a long time. Finally he looked up.

"I'm sorry. Grandfather must have put a lock spell on this book that only he can remove. I guess he thought that the spells in here were too powerful for others to see. I...I'm sorry. I can't open it. I can't reverse the transformation spell."

# MUSICIANS OF FREYFALL

I F CAT COULD HAVE BANGED HER FISTS AND
yelled, she would have. As it was, all she could do was
meow. It didn't help.

"I'm sorry," Garth said miserably.

He was sorry. What good did that do? Cat turned her
back and stared at the wall. Silence fell like a heavy curtain.

"It won't be forever," Garth said. "When Grandfather
gets back, I'll ask him. He's sure to know how to reverse the
spell and turn you back into a girl." He was quiet for a
moment, then added in a low voice. "He can't think worse
of me than he does already."

She refused to feel sorry for him. She kept her back
turned.

"While we wait, we can look for your father."

Despite herself, Cat's ears pricked up.

"Other musicians may know where he lives. We can ask
them. I know where musicians gather."

*I'm sure you do,* Cat thought sourly. *You probably spend all your time with them rather than learning how to make spells that work.*

Garth's voice quickened into eagerness. "Starting tomorrow, we can spend all week searching for him. By the time Grandfather returns and transforms you, we'll have found him. In the meantime…" His voice faded. He cleared his throat. "I hope you won't mind too much being a cat."

Cat hoped so too.


BY MORNING, she knew that she did mind. A lot. Oh, she could manage her legs without tripping over them now. And they fed her well enough, Mistress Grove and Ellen – more milk, bits of fish, scraps of meat. Cooked meat. They'd tried to give her raw liver, but she'd backed away in such horror that they'd substituted leftover pieces of the Spellmans' dinner.

"I've never known a cat turn up its nose at liver before," Ellen said.

"They can be picky eaters, cats. I had one once would eat liver for weeks, then act as though he couldn't stand the stuff," Mistress Grove replied.

"Still, beggars can't be choosers."

"Oh well. It doesn't hurt to give puss what she wants. And Master Garth seems fond of it, and it's little enough pleasure he gets with Master Spellman always after him to work harder."

"He works hard enough at his lute."

"When he's allowed to," Mistress Grove agreed.

After dinner, Cat curled up in a corner and slept. She was tired enough to sleep anywhere, and at least she was indoors, not huddled in some doorway.

In her dreams, she sat with her grandmother in the kitchen at Ashdale, then walked through dew-fresh grass as she herded the cows to pasture. Waking to four legs, fur, and paws was a shock.

Ellen was hard at work, stirring up the embers in the fireplace and adding wood to the stove, but Cat could tell it was still early. The sun just touched the window ledge, and the birds sang lustily. Cat cocked her ears. She had never heard such loud birdsong. But then, she had never heard with a cat's ears before, she reminded herself. Her stomach tightened.

Garth entered. "Freyn's Day."

Ellen started. "You're up early, Master Garth."

"Yes, well, I've a lot to do today. Would you please tell Mother I'll be gone for a while?"

"Your breakfast –"

"I'll help myself to some bread and cheese and eat on the way. Is there anything for the cat to eat before we leave?"

"You're taking it with you?"

"Yes."

Ellen shrugged, as though resigned to his strange ways, and placed a plate with bread crumbs moistened by bacon fat in front of Cat. Cat devoured them, then licked her whiskers.

"Finished?" Garth asked. "Let's be on our way, then."

Ellen laughed. "You talk to that cat as though it understands every word you speak."

Garth's face reddened. "Yes, well... We'd best be off," he said, not looking at the young woman.

Cat padded after him through the hall and out into the quiet, slumbering street. In the stillness, the rush of the waterfall could be heard even at this distance. She raised her eyes to the water, a veil of golden mist in the early morning sun.

Garth noticed the direction of her gaze. "It's almost magical, isn't it? Sometimes I think I'd like nothing better than to travel, but I know I'd miss the falls if I did. It's especially beautiful at this time of day. I love the early morning, don't you? It's so fresh, somehow, so full of possibilities. Then, by the end of the day, everything's gone flat, and I haven't done any of the things I wanted to do."

He sighed and looked down at her. "We didn't really have to be out this soon. The musicians won't start to gather until noon. I wanted to be away before Mother woke up. Not that she'd try to stop me from going out, but she'd feel guilty and worried about what Grandfather would say. We'll just wander around for a while."

Wander they did. Cat found the city fascinating, seen through a cat's eyes, heard through a cat's ears, smelled through a cat's nose. Her senses were so much keener, and there was so much going on at ground level: caterpillars crawling among the cobblestones, ants scurrying over them, dog smells left at every gate and carriage wheel, the tails of mice and rats flickering out of sight as she approached. Her eyes followed the tails with sharp interest. Her tail twitched.

Were her cat instincts taking over? Cat flinched and drew nearer to Garth.

He looked down. "It's getting busy. Maybe I should carry you."

It *was* getting busy. Street vendors were out, shops were open, carts rumbled by continuously, and people strolled or hurried past in a forest of legs. Cat didn't object when Garth picked her up.

"We'll go to The Laughing Lute soon," he told her. "It's a tavern where musicians go to meet other musicians and try out their new songs. There are two others just as popular with them, but The Lute's closest."

Was it a place she had visited already? It didn't sound familiar, but she had entered so many taverns in her fruitless quest, even here on the east bank, that their names drifted through her head like the mist of the falls, impossible to hold.

Garth walked slowly, pausing now and then to examine the goods on display. Cat watched everything with alert interest from the security of his arms. They stopped once to listen to a woman sing. Her voice was rich and powerful, but Cat didn't think she conveyed the mood of the songs very well.

Garth seemed to agree. "You sing much better than she does," he told her. A man standing next to him gave him a startled look, then edged away.

It was beginning to get hot. Garth shifted Cat to one arm and wiped his face with a handkerchief. He sighed as he replaced the handkerchief and resumed his former hold. He'd been carrying her for over an hour now. Cat thought for a moment, then wriggled free of his arms. Climbing his chest to his shoulder, she wound herself around his neck. Her perch felt precarious. She tightened her grip.

"That's a good idea, cat, but loosen your claws a bit, will you?"

Reluctantly, she did so.

Wearing Cat like a fur collar, Garth wove his way down the street, heading for The Laughing Lute. Then, abruptly, he halted.

Cat sighed. The stall in front of them displayed musical instruments. At this rate, they'd never reach the tavern. Her eyes scanned the lutes, whistles, harps, reeds, flutes –

She gasped. Dug her claws into Garth's flesh.

"Ow! What are you doing?" Garth reached up to loosen Cat's claws, but she didn't notice. Without thinking, she jumped from his shoulder and landed on the stall beside a carved wooden flute.

"Get that cat off my stall!" shouted the owner, a heavy-set man with a bushy dark beard. "What's it doing there?"

"She's a musical cat," Garth said absently, looking from Cat to the flute and back again.

"A musical cat? What do you mean? It might damage my merchandise. Get it off."

Garth scooped up Cat with one hand and fingered the flute with the other. "How much are you charging for this?"

The man's anger disappeared more quickly than a burst bubble. "Two gold pieces."

Cat's eyes widened. Had Kenton paid that price for her flute?

Garth shook his head. "It's not worth that much."

"It's a fine flute. Look at the carving. I've rarely seen such exquisite work. And it has a beautiful tone. Here. Why don't you try it?"

"I don't have two gold pieces. Few people do, for a flute." Garth turned to leave.

"One gold and eight silver, and may Freyn forgive me for cheating myself."

Garth turned back, but shook his head again. "It's still too high."

Disappointment stabbed Cat. But he was right, of course. It *was* too much. Far too much. She gave the flute one last loving glance, then averted her eyes.

"One and seven, then, and that only because I can see you have music in your soul. You and your cat."

"One and two."

"May Freyn protect my old age, one and six, and that's my final offer."

They finally settled on a price of one and three. Garth rummaged, first in the purse at his belt, then in his pockets. He came up ten coppers short. The stall owner waved a magnanimous hand. "For you, a music lover, I'll forgive the difference. Enjoy the flute."

"For the price, I'd better," Garth said dryly. He lifted Cat to his shoulders, then picked up the flute.

"It *is* the flute, isn't it?" he asked as they walked up the street. "The one you sold to buy your passage?"

Cat meowed, the only answer she could make. She couldn't mistake the mouse, curled up among the leaves, or the fawn's head, raised alertly. But Garth shouldn't have spent so much on it. She hadn't asked him to. Had she?

Garth stopped in front of a small building made of whitewashed stone, with a green door and shutters. The sign above the door bore the picture of a man holding a lute in one hand and a mug in the other. Cat was sure she'd have remembered the sign if she'd been here before. The door was open, and the sounds of music and laughter welcomed them.

Cat's eyes automatically adjusted to the light, which seemed dim after the midday sun outside. She saw a wooden bar at one end, with a smiling, round pudding of a man behind it. Most of the company was seated at a long trestle table that stood in front of the sole window. Cat counted twelve men and two women. One man, to the accompaniment of guffaws and catcalls, strummed a lute and sang. Cat wasn't sure whether she'd have laughed or blushed – or both – at the words of the song, if she'd still been a girl.

The singer ended with a dramatic flourish and a grand bow. "And that," he announced solemnly, "is the song I intend to enter in the contest and sing before Queen Elira and the wizards."

Howls of glee greeted his words.

"I can just see their faces."

"You'd be booted into the street."

"Even you would never dare, Mel."

"No?" Mel asked, a devilish smile lurking around his lips.

There was more laughter. More protests. "It would never get past the selection committee."

"Too bad," someone commented. "I'd love to be a fly on the wall at the council if Mel did sing it."

A man spotted Garth. "Ho, Garth. How would your grandfather react to Mel's song?"

Garth grinned. "I don't think he'd be amused."

Mel waved a hand. "Come join us."

The fair-haired woman sitting at the end of the bench moved over and Garth sat down. He carefully placed the flute on the table before him, drawing murmurs of admiration and cries of delight. Without being asked, the tavern keeper brought another mug and someone poured ale into it. Cat jumped to the floor. How easy it was, with her new muscles.

"What's this?" asked the woman beside Garth. "You've got a new cat as well as a new flute?"

"Yes."

"What do you call it?"

"Just...cat."

The fair woman laughed. "How original. You've got a real flair for names, that's plain to see."

"It doesn't match your usual gift for wordsmithing, Garth," Mel commented.

Cat looked up at Garth, surprised. Did he make songs as well as play them, then?

"Can you spare any scraps for her, Rolf?" Garth asked the landlord.

"Of course, lad. And a meal for yourself as well?"

Garth shook his head. "I'm not hungry, thanks."

Cat thought of the last few coins he'd scraped from the

bottom of his pockets to pay for the flute, and ignored the plate set in front of her, despite the smell of hot meat pie that had been tickling her nostrils since they'd entered the tavern. Garth gave her an anxious look. She ignored it, too. He sighed and sat toying with his drink while the talk flowed on around him.

The talk was all about the competition. Despite the jokes and laughter, it was clear that they all, including Mel, took it very seriously indeed and intended to enter.

"Who among us do you truly think will be chosen?" asked a dark-haired, dark-eyed man who'd been sipping his ale and watching the others with a sardonic eye.

"All of us, of course, Whalen," said the fair-haired woman. "Aren't we the best musicians in Freyfall? The best in all Freya?"

Cheers. Laughter.

"I'll drink to that," shouted a freckled youth with a mop of carroty curls. Glasses clinked to the sound of more cheers.

Whalen shook his head. "I've heard that only five will be chosen. And you're living in a fool's dream if you think the contest will be judged solely on merit."

"What do you mean, Whalen?" Mel demanded.

"The council is designed to improve relations among the three lands and draw the wizards and wise women closer together."

"We know that, Whalen," said a man with a straggly brown beard. "What's your point?"

"My point is that the judges are going to want to make sure at least some Uglessians and Islandians are included among the winners."

"But there aren't any Islandians in Freya, are there?" someone asked uncertainly.

"No Islandians, maybe," Whalen conceded, "but there's plenty of Uglessians. We give them our rain. We give them bushels of coins for their kala roots. Now we'll give up the chance to make names for ourselves. It's time we stopped being so generous."

There was a small silence. People exchanged glances. A few murmured agreement. Then a lean, middle-aged man with a quiet face shook his head. "You've not been to Uglessia, Whalen. I have. We may have shared some rain and paid fair prices for their kala, but I'd hate to try to live as they must. Go there, then repeat your comments."

An auburn-haired young woman tossed her head. "Anyway, I don't believe the queen's jurors won't be fair. I'm not afraid of any competition. You're too gloomy, Whalen."

The tension eased. Someone called for another flagon of ale. The chatter and laughter resumed. Cat stared hard at Garth's back, willing him to ask about her father. As though feeling her gaze, he turned and gave her a reassuring smile. She sighed and settled down to wait, half dozing in a patch of sunlight.

Through a haze of sleep, she became aware of a lull in the talk, broken by Garth's tentative voice. "Does anyone know a minstrel named Gayland Bellmore?"

Cat sat up abruptly, instantly alert.

"Bellmore," said the man with the straggly beard. "The name sounds vaguely familiar. What does he play? Does he live in Freyfall?"

"He wanders the roads. He sings and plays the lute, but knows other instruments as well. We think he's in Freyfall now because of the contest."

"So is every musician in Freya," Whalen muttered.

"We?" asked the fair-haired woman.

"A...friend and I."

"I've got it," said the man with the beard, snapping his fingers. "I met him on the road, somewhere near... Now, where was it? Applegarth, I think. A yellow-haired man, with itching feet. He said he never stayed long in any one place. About your age, Sander," he said, nodding to the middle-aged man. "A merry fellow he was, with a gift for making up funny songs on the spur of the moment. Pleasant company. He made the time go quickly as we walked along."

Cat's heart was pounding.

"I met a man of that description once, though I never heard his name," Sander said. "He may well have a chance in the competition. He had a good clear voice, as I recall, and a fine touch on the lute. He was travelling with a woman with a rich alto voice. Lucia, I think she was called. A beauty, too, though too thin for my taste."

Cat stared at him.

"Do either of you know where he is now?" Garth asked.

The younger man shook his head. Sander said, "Sorry, lad. I haven't seen him for over a year."

"You could try The Pheasant's Nest or The Lucky Lady," Mel suggested.

Garth nodded. "Thank you. I will."

Talk of the competition resumed. Cat sank onto her haunches and stared sightlessly at the square of sunshine in front of her. Her father...with a woman. Well, why not? It shouldn't matter. But it did. It changed everything.

Immersed in her thoughts, she didn't realize that Garth had risen until he picked her up and settled her on his shoulders. He nodded his farewells.

"Wait, Garth, I'll walk a ways with you." Mel tossed some coppers onto the table and stood. They emerged into the hot, busy street. Cat was surprised to see that the sun had already begun its slow slide into the west.

"Do you know a wizard named Danlo Wishbe?" Mel asked, shortening his strides to match Garth's shorter legs.

"Master Wishbe? I've met him. He's one of the most prominent wizards in town. Why?"

"He was around to see me, asking some funny questions."

"Funny questions? What do you mean?"

"Well, first he said he'd heard I had quite a gift for writing comic songs. Very complimentary about it, he was. Then he asked whether I planned to enter the competition. He didn't seem to realize that it's one thing to enter and quite another to win." Mel snorted.

"Of course you'll win, Mel," Garth assured him.

"Thanks, Garth, but we both know there's no 'of course' about it. Things got stranger after that. He asked me how much money I make – which isn't very much, but I didn't tell him that. Then he wanted to know how I felt about these foreigners taking our jobs and our rain. I told him some of my best friends are Uglessians. It's not true, but I don't like talk like that. He left, looking as black as thunder." Mel paused, but Garth said nothing.

"I thought I'd ask you about the man, since it all seemed a bit odd to me."

"I don't really know him that well," Garth said.

"Your grandfather probably does, though. Could you ask him?"

Cat felt Garth stiffen. "It...might be awkward," he said carefully. "They respect each other's abilities, and sometimes confer about magic. I don't think Grandfather would appreciate me asking."

Mel shrugged. "It probably isn't important. I was just curious." He grinned at the boy. "So what about you? Are you planning to try your hand at singing before the queen?"

"Me?" Garth's voice went high with surprise.

"Why not? You sing and play well, and you've written some delightful songs. I still remember your 'Freyfall Mist.'"

Garth's head was bent. "I'm not a musician," he mumbled.

"No? You could have fooled me. Well, here's where I turn. Freyn's Day to you. And to you, cat." He gave Cat a quick pat and left, waving a friendly hand.

Garth stared after him for a long moment before walking on.

# THREADMORE STREET

SAUSAGE. FRYING ONIONS. MEAT PIES. FISH. CAT sniffed hungrily as they passed one food stall after another. Why, oh why, had she been too proud to eat when she had the chance? Her stomach rumbled.

Garth emerged from the fog he'd entered after Mel's departure. "Hungry? Don't worry. We'll go home and eat dinner now. We can go to The Pelican's Nest afterwards."

But Mistress Spellman had other plans. She was hovering in the hall when they arrived, and greeted her son with mixed relief and anger.

"At last! Where have you been?"

"Out."

Mistress Spellman's voice sharpened. "I realize that. Where?"

Garth shrugged. "Around." After a moment, he added, "Mostly at The Laughing Lute."

"I might have known. Garth...didn't your grandfather

leave work for you to do while he's gone?"

"Yes." He bent and placed Cat on the floor, his face hidden.

"And don't you think you should do it?"

"I have something else to do. It's important."

"More important than how your grandfather will feel when he finds you've neglected your work?"

"Don't worry. He'll be angry at me, not you."

"Garth!"

Cat winced at the hurt she heard in the woman's voice. Without thinking, she went to her and rubbed against her legs.

Mistress Spellman glanced down at her, then up again at her son. Her face hardened. "You will not leave this house again until you've completed everything your grandfather told you to do."

Garth, who had flushed and lowered his head a moment before, now jerked it up. "But –"

"No buts. You will not move a foot from this house until you're finished."

"But I have to –"

"You have to complete your tasks. Now –" she took a deep breath "go wash up for dinner."

"Mother –"

"Garth, that will do. Go." She bent and lifted Cat into her arms. She was trembling slightly. "I'll take the cat to the kitchen for its dinner."

Later, Cat crept into the study. Garth had left the door open a crack for her. He sat behind the desk, staring into empty space. Cat had to meow loudly before he noticed her.

"Oh, cat. I'm sorry. I guess we can't go out tonight. In fact, I'm not sure when we can. It will take ages to get through all that Grandfather left for me. But don't fret," he added, giving her a quick smile. "If it takes too long, I'll just sneak out. Though..." His smile faded. He looked away. "I shouldn't have spoken to Mother like that."

Cat agreed. She tried to tell him so with another loud meow.

Garth ignored her. Sighing, he bent his head and began to read. Cat curled up on the rug and gnawed at her own worries. After a while, she slept.

For the next few days, Garth concentrated grimly on his studies. Cat was impressed by how hard he could work, though she did notice him thrust his book aside once and scribble musical notes on a piece of paper, humming the tune softly. Cat spent the time exploring when she wasn't dozing in the study.

The house was a long, narrow, four-storied building, kept spotless by Mistress Fairway's sharp eyes and sharper tongue. The servants' quarters were on the top floor. There were three servants besides the housekeeper, Cat discovered: the cook, Mistress Grove, who seemed the only person in the household unaffected by Mistress Fairway's acidic ways, the maid Ellen, and another maid named Della. Bedchambers for family and guests were on the third floor, which left the bottom two levels to be occupied by the kitchen, the dining room, the study, a small sitting room where Mistress Spellman spent much of her time, and three larger, more formal sitting rooms.

Cat roamed the house at will, delighting in her new body, which allowed her to slip through narrow spaces and leap onto surfaces five times her height. She especially loved to sit on window ledges and gaze out onto the back garden, one of the few green spaces she'd found in this city of stone and brick.

Mistress Fairway found her one day, sitting on a windowsill in a large, ornate sitting room that echoed with nothing but silence.

"Shoo! You don't belong here."

Secure in Mistress Spellman's protection, Cat gave the housekeeper a disdainful look and turned her back on her. For a moment, she thought she'd gone too far. Then, with a loud, "Tsk! Wait till the master returns," the woman stalked away.

Wait till the master returns. That's just what Cat was doing. Waiting for him to return. Waiting for him to turn her back into herself.

*What if he can't?*

She shook her head. Shook it again. Tried to shake the thought away.

In the meantime, she waited for Garth, and brooded.

Finally, in mid-afternoon of the fourth day, Garth slammed his book shut and sat back with a sigh of relief. Cat's ears pricked.

"There. That's done. Come on." Garth set off in search of his mother. Cat padded beside him. They found Mistress Spellman in the small sitting room, embroidering a linen shift. Her smooth, slender hands moved with practised skill, creating a dancing parade of lilies of the valley and bleeding hearts just above the hem.

"I'm finished," Garth announced.

Mistress Spellman put the shift down and smiled at him. "Good for you. Your grandfather will be proud of you." She was looking very pretty today, Cat thought, in her rose dress and with the sun adding a rich gloss to her hair, braided as usual, on top of her head.

Garth snorted.

"Well, *I'm* proud of you anyway. See what you can do when you concentrate. A week's worth of work done in less than four days."

"I'm going out now."

Her smile faded. "It's getting on towards dinnertime."

"I'll grab some bread and cheese to eat as I go. Come on, cat."

His mother laughed. "You take that cat with you everywhere. Why don't you give her a name?"

"I...it would seem wrong, when I don't know her real – That is, I... Anyway, she won't be here much longer."

Mistress Spellman studied her son's face. "And you don't want to give her a name because you think that would make it harder to give her up?" she asked gently. "Garth, I don't think your grandfather will make you turn her out. Not if you tell him how much she means to you. And I'll speak to him too."

"It's not... Anyway, he wouldn't listen."

"Garth –"

"I have to go." Garth bolted out the door and down the stairs to the kitchen. Cat trailed after him, annoyed. Why didn't Garth just tell his mother the truth? Life would be so much simpler. After all, he was going to tell his grandfather.

Or was he? Cat stopped, arrested by a sudden doubt. Garth so obviously feared his grandfather – or, at least, his grandfather's scorn. Would he really confess to having made such a horrible blunder?

Of course he would.

Wouldn't he?

She heard him call, "Cat!" Slowly, she descended the rest of the stairs.

"Here, you'd better eat something before we go." He thrust a plate in front of her.

"You do talk to that cat as if it was human," Ellen said, grinning at him.

Garth muttered something Cat couldn't catch. She ate quickly, then followed him outside.

"We'll go to The Pelican's Nest," Garth said, settling her on his shoulders. "It's on the central island."

The streets were still crowded, and it took some time for Garth to weave a path through them. As they approached The Pelican's Nest, Cat realized she'd been there before. But that had been at mid-morning, when few customers were present. The drowsy tavern was transformed. She winced as they entered the dim room. *Why* did people in Freyfall have to talk so loudly? And sing so loudly? And laugh so loudly?

The benches were full, but a young man seated at a corner table waved at them. "Garth! Come join me. I've a new song. You'll love it."

Garth grinned as he squeezed onto the end of the bench. "I hope it's an improvement on your last effort, Brandon."

"What do you mean? That song was inspired."

"Inspired by what? Wine?"

Brandon spluttered. Cat jumped to the floor, resigning herself to a long night.

It *was* a long night. Worse, it was fruitless. Cat had to give Garth credit: he went from table to table, asking whether anyone knew Gayland Bellmore. Some said the name was familiar. One man even claimed he'd seen him recently. Cat's heart leaped. When asked about the musician's present whereabouts, however, the man shook his head.

"Never mind, cat," Garth said as they left the tavern and walked down the dark, almost deserted streets. "We'll find him. We'll check out The Lucky Lady tomorrow."

It's easy enough for *you* to be cheerful, Cat thought. *You* don't care how long it takes to find my father. Searching for him gives you an excuse to go from tavern to tavern, listening to music, talking about music. And you're probably hoping it will be a while before your grandfather returns and you have to admit your mistake. *You* don't care that I'm a cat.

She'd be better off if she'd never gone to the wizard's house, never met Garth Spellman.

Better to be wandering the streets, hungry? Huddled in some doorway, trying to sleep on cold, hard stones?

Cat shivered. Maybe not. Maybe it was better to be a cat with a home than a homeless girl.

The Lucky Lady was located on the west bank of the river, a stone's throw away from a building that Garth identified as the palace the queen stayed in when she was in Freyfall. Cat surveyed it with interest. It stood at the end of a large square, and every line sang with elegance, from its delicately carved columns to its high arched windows and the lacy pattern on the iron railings of the balconies. But there was nothing elegant or delicate about the two heavily armed soldiers who stood in front of the door, doing their best to look like stone statues.

It was still early when they reached The Lucky Lady, and the tavern was relatively empty. By noon, however, it was packed. Cat crouched in a corner, away from the tramp of feet going to and from the bar. She watched Garth leave his spot on a bench and approach a group of newcomers. With this crowd, he'd never recover his vacated seat. Not that he'd care as long as there was music and the talk of music.

Garth's body tensed. Excitement leapt into his face.

Cat streaked to his side.

"We were in this very tavern, two nights back," a man with a round belly and deep bass voice was saying. "Talking about the competition, as who isn't these days? Stayed till the place closed, then found our paths lay in the same direction. He's rented a room till after the competition, same as me and many another minstrel. He stopped at a house before me, nine or ten blocks from here. A house with a blue door, as near as I could tell given the dark and the ale I'd drunk. On Threadmore Street, it was."

"Thank you," Garth said. He looked down as Cat sprang into his arms. From there, she climbed onto his shoulders.

The houses around The Lucky Lady were fat and smug. But as they approached Threadmore Street, the streets grew poorer and dingier, the houses smaller and shabbier. Threadmore Street itself was short and narrow, with houses that sagged dispiritedly against each other. Even a horse plodding down the road looked tired, as did its rider.

Garth walked slowly, scrutinizing each house carefully as he passed. He came to a stop in front of a building with a peeling, faded blue door, and lifted his hand to turn the knob.

Cat dug her claws into his shoulder.

"Ow! Cat, stop it."

Her claws remained extended.

"What do you think you're doing? Do you want to find your father or don't you?"

She did. Of course she did. Then why this sudden panic?

Garth lifted his hand again. She let out a loud, piteous meow. He dropped it.

"I don't understand. For six days now, you've told me, as plainly as though you could talk, that you're in a hurry to find your father. Now that we have found him, you don't want to meet him. It doesn't make sense."

She knew it didn't. She meowed again.

"Do you want to wait until you're a girl again? Is that it? I suppose it makes sense." He paused, then added, "I can't say I'm looking forward to telling a man I've turned his daughter into a cat. All right. We'll go home now, and return after Grandfather has transformed you."

# THE FIGHTING COCK

THE HOUSE WAS STILL AND DARK, EXCEPT FOR the embers glowing in the kitchen's fireplace. Cat stared at them.

Why, oh why, had she been so reluctant to meet her father? She had come to Freyfall to find him. She had hunted for him for days. For weeks. So why the sudden panic that had attacked her on his doorstep?

*Was* it because she was wearing a cat's body?

No.

Cat sank her head onto her paws. The truth was, she was afraid. Afraid that her father wanted nothing to do with her. After all, he'd left her twelve years ago. He hadn't seen her since then. And what about this woman he'd been with? This Lucia.

If only there were some way she could discover more about him before she presented herself.

Her ears pricked. She sat up.

She could return to Threadmore Street and spy on him.

Cats could slip into places no human could go.

The window was open a crack, letting in the cool night breeze. Could she get through it?

She leapt onto the windowsill. Her head was a bit of a problem, but she managed to squeeze it though, grazing it slightly. The rest was easy.

The garden delayed her a few minutes. It was full of the whirring of insect wings and the smells of moist earth and blossoms. The grass felt soft and dew-fresh on her pavement-weary paws.

But she had a mission. Resolutely, she headed for the rear of the garden and squirmed through the bars of the iron railing. There. She was off.

It was a long journey. She hadn't realized just how long, but then she'd been riding on Garth's shoulders for much of her earlier trip. A half moon gave enough light for her new cat's eyes, but she started at shadows several times, and jumped to one side, heart pounding, when a large black cat leapt from a window ledge and stood confronting her. Was it friendly or hostile? She didn't wait to find out. She ran.

Following remembered smells as much as familiar land-marks, she found Gayland's house. She hunted for open windows, but there were none, at least none that she could reach.

Now what? Cat sat on her haunches on the cobblestones and stared at the faded blue door. She was no closer to seeing her father than she had been in Master Spellman's house in east Freyfall. And she was much less comfortable.

She would have to wait until morning. With a sigh, she

sank down in a dense shadow across the street, prepared for a long night.

She was woken from a fitful doze by the thump of a closing door. A man emerged from the house with the blue door. Cat watched, body tense, as he settled a cloak around his shoulders and set off briskly down the road. Was it...? Could it be...? She crept after him, keeping to the shadows.

He walked for some time before stopping in front of a tavern. Candlelight glowed feebly from behind closed shutters, the only sign of light Cat could see in the dark, deserted street.

The man opened the door and went inside. Cat hesitated. Should she follow? Above her head, something creaked. She jumped, then looked up to see a sign flapping in the breeze. It bore a picture of a large rooster, bristling, ready to fight, and the words, "The Fighting Cock."

The door didn't close firmly. It was easy to push it open and slip inside.

The room was dimly lit by a few smoking candles. A small brown nut of a man sat on a stool behind the bar. Aside from him, the tavern was empty except for a solitary patron sitting at a corner table where the shadows lay deepest. Cat watched the man she'd followed join him.

She wrinkled her nose, assaulted by smells of stale beer and unwashed bodies. She was tempted to leave. But if the person she'd trailed really *was* her father... She crept forward along the dark shelter of the wall until she was close enough to hear the two speak.

"You choose meeting places that are...less than appetizing, shall we say," said the newcomer, looking around him. He had a pleasant voice, a voice that seemed to laugh and sing. Cat's breath caught in her throat. Surely, surely, this was her father!

The other man confirmed it. "Don't complain, Bellmore. This is a good place if you don't want to be seen."

"Hmm. I can see why you might not want to be seen with me."

"What do you mean?" the other asked sharply.

"I've been doing some thinking since our last conversation. After this is all over, I'm not going to be very popular, am I? The consequences may be...drastic."

"Nonsense. You'll be seen as a singer whose sense of a good jest got the better of him, that's all."

"A singer who has deceived the queen's musicians – and therefore the queen herself. A singer who's done his best – or his worst – to wreck the queen's plans. That might be viewed as treason."

Treason? What was this talk of treason? Cat stared at the two men.

"Queen Elira has no right to entangle us yet further with Islandians and Uglessians," Gayland's companion hissed, jutting his head forward into the light. Cat made out a pointed beard, but that was all. The rest of his face was hidden by a deep hood.

Gayland shrugged. "That's no concern of mine."

"It's the concern of all decent Freyans who care about their country." The man's voice rose. He lowered it with an obvious effort. "But of course your concern is the money we're paying you. Is that what this is all about? Are you demanding more?"

Cat could have clawed the man for the sneer in his voice, but Gayland seemed unperturbed. "I could use more, especially now," he admitted.

"I've told you, you'll receive five gold pieces after your report tonight, and five more after your next report. The rest will come when you've finished the job."

"And been locked up for doing it, probably. The money won't do me much good then."

"I've told you we'll look after you."

"So you have. Forgive me, but I find this desire not to be seen in my company less than reassuring."

"Of course we can't be seen together, fool. Too many people know me. But we'll make sure you're safe afterwards."

"Hmm. Who is this 'we' you keep referring to? I've only ever met you."

"That doesn't matter. Now," he leaned forward, his voice sinking to a whisper, "how is the song coming along?"

Cat took a step closer to hear. Her claws scraped the floor. She froze.

"What's that?" The hooded head swung around. "Oh, just a cat. Wilf should keep the cursed things out of here."

"Probably sneaked in looking for scraps." Gayland reached down. "Here, puss." Cat stared at his hand. "Come on, now. I don't bite." Slowly she approached, and felt his fingers stroke her fur. His touch was gentle.

The other man hissed. "Leave that creature alone and answer my question."

Gayland ignored him. "Wilf," he called to the landlord, "do you have any scraps for a stray cat?"

"Don't feed strays."

"How about for a few coppers?" Gayland tossed some coins across the room. They landed on the bar. Wilf grunted. A moment later, a plate was put in front of Cat. The meat on it looked like the rejects from last week's stew, and her stomach was too jumpy for hunger. She ate it anyway. It was a gift. A gift from her father.

"If you've quite finished with that cat, I did ask you a question," the hooded man said, his voice quivering with barely suppressed anger.

"Ah yes. The song. Which song?"

The man's hands clenched. "You know which song."

"Do I? But there will be two songs, surely – unless, of course, you think a song that insults our guests will be acceptable to those judging the competition."

The hands unclenched. "Obviously you will need another song for the judges."

"Obviously. And that one, my friend, will have to be very good indeed. Do you have any idea how many musicians – good musicians, at that – plan to enter the contest?"

"I daresay. But it's the other song that worries me."

"I'd advise you to worry about both, my friend. If the first's not good enough, the second won't be sung. Then where will you be? No cat among the pigeons."

"Then make sure both are good," the other man snapped.

"But of course," Gayland murmured.

"How far have you progressed?"

"I have a few ideas. The beginnings of a melody."

"Is that all? The council is less than a month away. The contest –"

"A little over three weeks away. I know."

"Then why this delay?"

"There's no delay. It takes time to compose a good song. Two good songs."

"You don't expect to be paid for this, do you? I need proof you can do it. What are these ideas of yours?"

"Ideas... I've toyed with a few, but the one I favour at the moment has to do with ursells."

"Ursells?"

"The mountain beasts that Uglessians milk and sheer and ride."

"I know what ursells are, fool. But what –"

"Uglessians think very highly of their ursells, I'm told, even call them their brothers and sisters. The songs and stories tell us that during our first contacts with the Uglessians, we were repulsed because they seemed totally grey, with their pale faces and dressed uniformly in undyed ursell wool. I thought I would – emphasize, shall we say – this resemblance. It's only a thought, of course," he added with a deprecating shrug.

There was a long silence. Finally, the hooded man nodded slowly. "It just might work." He held out his hand.

Cat saw the gleam of gold before Gayland shoved the coins into his pocket. The other rose. "I'll meet you in a week's time. I expect you to have the completed song."

"Here?"

"No. The Merry Jug. Do you know where it is?"

"I'll find it."

The man turned to go.

"Wait," Gayland said.

He turned back. "What is it now?"

"After I've sung my song and the Uglessians are suitably insulted...what then?"

"I've told you, we'll look after you."

"I don't mean... What do you expect to happen at the council? After the council?"

"I expect the Uglessians to leave and the Islandians to follow. I expect there will be no closer alliances with them."

"Nothing more? Nothing more...extreme?"

"Of course not. Anyway, I thought all you cared about was your pay. What more need concern you?"

Gayland's mouth quirked. "What more indeed?" His eyes followed the man's departing back, then continued to stare into space. Cat crouched motionless, watching his face. Finally, he stirred.

"Well," he said softly to himself. He looked down at Cat. "Fed, are you? I trust you're feeling better for it, and feeling better than I am right now. I must admit to a slight queasiness in my stomach."

He bent, scratched behind Cat's ears, then rose abruptly and walked out of The Fighting Cock.

# WIZARD'S HOMECOMING

DAWN WAS FILLING THE EASTERN SKY BY the time Cat dragged herself home. Not home, she reminded herself. This was Garth's home. Master Spellman's home. Her home was far away, in distant Frey-under-Hill, where an old stone house stood in an ash-filled meadow, where people thought about cows and crops and preparing meals, not about...not about...

Not about treason.

What did it matter? What did the concerns of queens and wizards have to do with her? Would any of those great folk have cared if she had starved in the streets?

What mattered was that Gayland Bellmore was kind. He had spent money to feed a stray cat. His hands were gentle.

But the hollow ache in her stomach persisted.

It was too much effort to jump onto the kitchen window ledge and squeeze inside. She sat on the grass in the narrow back garden, watching the sky turn from pink to gold to blue, listening to two bluebirds sing from their perch in the apple tree in the corner.

The door opened and Garth stuck his head out. His face lit up when he saw Cat.

"There you are." He came over and sat beside her. "I was worried sick when I couldn't find you. I thought... But you wouldn't go, would you? I mean...you do know everything will be all right when Grandfather returns, don't you?" He peered at her anxiously, then sighed. "I do wish you could talk."

Cat didn't. To talk was the last thing she wanted right now.

"I suppose you came out here to enjoy the grass and trees. Freyfall must seem noisy and crowded and lacking in green places to someone from Frey-under-Hill." He fell silent, head cocked. Dreams flickered across his face. "I sometimes think, if I listened hard enough, I could capture birdsong in music. A flute, perhaps." He shot Cat a guilty look. "I tried your flute. I didn't mean to, but... You're lucky. At least, you will be once you can play it again."

He sighed. "But I shouldn't be thinking about music. Now that we've found your father, I should concentrate on magic. It might appease Grandfather, and Freyn knows he'll need appeasing. He'll be furious when he discovers I've turned you into a cat." He rose. "Coming for breakfast?"

Cat shook her head. She wasn't hungry.

She stayed outside most of the day, staring into space. She only went in when Garth, looking worried, came to fetch her for dinner.

"Is something wrong?"

She shook her head. Even if she could have spoken, she wouldn't have told him. She wouldn't have told anyone.

Garth gazed at her unhappily. "I...it must be hard being a cat. I'm sorry. But it won't last much longer. Grandfather will be home tomorrow."

That was obvious. The next day, the servants bustled about, dusting furniture that, to Cat's eyes, looked dust-free, scrubbing floors that were already spotless. The house smelled of spice cake and roast lamb. Cat's appetite revived. She hung around the kitchen, sniffing hungrily and getting underfoot, until shooed away by the exasperated cook.

She went to the study then and lay under the open window, watching Garth through half-closed eyes. He was making a valiant effort to concentrate, but started at every unexpected noise. When horse hooves clopped down the street, he jumped to his feet, only to sink back into his chair with a sigh of relief when the horse clattered on past. By mid-afternoon, Cat's nerves were as raw as newly scraped skin.

Shortly before dinner, Cat heard a carriage approach. It stopped long enough for a passenger to alight. Garth rose, his face white. The front door opened and closed. Garth took a shaky breath, then walked into the hall. Cat crept after him and peered out.

A tall, lean man had just entered. He moved with the ease of youth, but there were wings of white in his dark hair, and his face was deeply lined. His eyes, under thin, arching eyebrows, were as black as the clothes he wore, and very sharp. Cat drew back.

"How are you, Father-in-law?" she heard Mistress Spellman ask.

A deep voice responded. "Well, thank you, Annette, or will be once I've washed the dust of the road off. And you? Has everything gone smoothly in my absence?"

"Yes, everything's been fine. And Garth's been working very hard," Annette Spellman said proudly.

"Really? Well, I'm glad to hear it."

Garth cleared his throat. "Grandfather, I need to talk to you."

"Not now, Garth. I want to wash, then sit down to a civilized meal. Anything you need to tell me can wait till afterwards."

Cat heard his footsteps on the stairs. Garth turned and gave her what he probably thought was a reassuring smile before he disappeared too. Cat resumed her place below the window. Her stomach was too tight for food.

Time dragged by. Cat listened to footsteps going from the kitchen to the dining room and back again. Finally, two sets approached the study. She sat up abruptly.

A knock came at the front door. A moment later, Cat heard Mistress Fairway's voice. "Master Wishbe to see you, sir."

A fractional pause, then Master Spellman said, "Very well. Please come to the study, Wishbe. I'll talk to you later, Garth."

"Grandfather –"

"Later, I said." There was iron in the voice.

Instinctively, Cat ducked behind the curtains just as Master Spellman ushered his guest into the room.

"Please sit down. May I offer you a glass of wine?"

"Thank you." Cat heard the sound of glasses, then the newcomer said, "I'm glad you're back. How was your trip?"

Cat's eyes narrowed. The voice sounded oddly familiar.

Master Spellman snorted. "Well enough, except that I'm not pleased with what I see at the College of Wizards. I may not always have agreed with Ben Grantwish, but at least he was an excellent wizard and made sure all the other teachers were too. The new Head is sadly mediocre."

"They should have chosen you."

*Where, oh where, had she heard that voice before?*

Master Spellman snorted again. "They'd scarcely choose a man they once kicked out."

There was a small silence, then Master Wishbe said softly, "Ah yes. I'd heard you'd been expelled. A dispute with a Uglessian girl, wasn't it?"

Cat's breath caught. There was no mistaking the hiss in the voice when it uttered the word "Uglessian." It belonged to the man with the deep hood, the man who'd met her father at The Fighting Cock.

# CONSPIRACY

I T WAS THE SAME MAN. SHE WAS SURE OF IT.
Through a fog of fear and confusion, Cat heard
Master Wishbe say, "As I heard the tale, you were
expelled because you disapproved of the College's decision to
accept Uglessian students."

A pause. Then Master Spellman said, "To be accurate, I
was expelled because of the actions I took to express my dis-
approval."

"Actions. Yes. That's why I'm here."

"What do you mean?" Master Spellman asked. Cat heard
him set his glass down with a sharp click.

"Freya is in a state of decline, just like the College. Some
of us think steps must be taken."

"What sort of steps?"

"Steps to stop this growing friendship with Uglessia and
Islandia. You can see what's come of it. Ever since Kerstin
Speller blackmailed the wizards into sending some of Freya's

rain to Uglessia, conditions have deteriorated. Oh, it's not so bad in good years. But when we hit a dry spell, as we have these last few years, we need all the rain Freyn sends us. And look what those Uglessians charge for the kala we've all grown so dependent on. It wouldn't be so bad if they'd all stick to their side of the mountains. But they don't. More and more of the Freynless creatures are coming here, taking work away from decent Freyans. And what do we do? We not only let them, we encourage them. It wasn't so bad when King Leander was alive.

"Oh, there were always those like the Spellers and Jem Brooks who were close to the foreigners, but at least the official policy was sensible. But ever since Queen Elira ascended the throne, things have gone from sad to desperate. And now, as though things weren't bad enough, we have this council foisted on us to draw us even closer to them – yes, and to Islandians too, who've always thought themselves too good for us. I tell you, Spellman, if something isn't done soon, we'll have Uglessians and Islandians telling us what to do."

Silence followed the wizard's heated words. Cat heard the hum of voices from another part of the house. Finally, Master Spellman spoke. "What are you going to do?"

The other man hesitated. "Are you with us?"

"Who is 'us'?"

"I can't tell you until I know you're with us."

"You must be fairly sure of my support or you wouldn't have told me this much."

"Yes."

Cat heard a chair pushed back. Feet walked towards the window. Stopped. She stared at a pair of black boots close beside her. Too close. She tried to draw back, retreat, but there was nowhere to go.

The boots remained motionless for a long time. At last Master Spellman said, his back to the room, "You are asking a great deal of me, to make such a commitment based on so little information."

"If you care about Freya –"

"I care a great deal about Freya. Still, I don't even know if your plan – you do have a plan?"

"Yes."

"I don't know whether your plan will work. Do you have any guarantee of success?"

"No," the other admitted grudgingly. "But it's a good plan. And none of us will be implicated if we fail."

Only my father, Cat thought bitterly.

"And the consequences of success?"

"Ah. The consequences of success. At the very least, the council will end in total failure and the Uglessians leave in anger and disgrace. At best –" his voice sank to a whisper Cat strained to hear, "the Islandians will retreat to the isolation of their islands, and Freyans will learn the folly of trusting their enemies. It is even possible we will have war – a war that will destroy the Uglessians once and for all."

Each word was an ice-cold needle, tipped with venom. Cat shuddered. The curtains stirred.

"What's that?" Master Wishbe asked sharply.

Cat froze.

"What?"

"The curtain. It moved just now."

A hand grasped the edge of the curtain, swished it aside. Cat crouched, staring at the black-clad legs in front of her.

*Run. Run.*

But her muscles had turned liquid. And Master Spellman blocked her way.

The window. Just above her. And open.

She willed her muscles into strength. Tensed.

Too late. Hands swooped down, gathered her up.

"A cat," Master Spellman said. "Well, well."

The other wizard grunted. "Just a cat. I keep running into them lately. Is this one yours?"

"Not as far as I know."

Master Wishbe hadn't recognized her. Cat's fear eased a little, but her heart still seemed to beat too hard for her small body.

"Well, what do you say, Spellman? Are you ready to join us?" Master Wishbe leaned forward, blue eyes intent. Everything about him was as precise and perfectly groomed as his pointed beard, Cat saw, from his even features to his impeccably tailored clothes.

The man holding Cat was very still. "You won't give me any more information?" he asked at last.

"After you've joined us."

"Very well. I'll join you."

"Swear in Freyn's name."

"Is that necessary? It seems a trifle – childish."

Master Wishbe's lips tightened. "We must safeguard ourselves against betrayal."

"All right. I swear in Freyn's name that I will not betray

your secrets. There. Will that do?"

Master Wishbe's face eased into a smile. "It will do very nicely. I knew we could count on you." He rose.

"You're leaving? Without telling me more?"

"That will come later."

"How much later? When do I meet my fellow conspirators?"

"I'll be in touch. And don't call us conspirators. We're involved in a sacred mission to save Freya."

"Of course."

The wizard ushered his guest to the front door and let him out. Cat wished he would let her go, but he didn't. Nor did he ease his grip so she could spring free.

"Grandfather?"

The man turned. "Ah, Garth. You wanted to talk to me, didn't you? Can it wait till tomorrow?"

Garth was standing halfway down the stairs. His eyes widened when he saw Cat.

"Cat?"

"Indeed it is a cat. I found it hiding in the study. You wouldn't happen to know how it got there, would you?"

"Yes. That's what I wanted to see you about." Garth gripped the banister so tightly his hand turned white. "Grandfather –"

Cat yowled. She clawed the hands holding her. They opened. She leapt to the floor. Raced up the stairs. Put her paw on Garth's leg and stared at him. He stared at her.

"A well-behaved cat, I can see," Konrad Spellman said sourly, examining his wounds. "Well? What is it about this cat that demands discussion? Apart from its manners, that is."

Garth swallowed. "I... This cat... She –"

Cat dug her claws into Garth's leg and shook her head violently.

Garth stopped, open-mouthed.

"Well?"

Garth gazed at Cat. She gazed back, eyes pleading. *Don't tell him,* she begged silently. *Don't tell him. It's not safe.*

Garth closed his mouth. He swallowed again, then said faintly, "I...sort of adopted her. She... May I keep her?"

"Is that what all this fuss was about? Keeping a cat? In Freyn's name, boy, grow up. You're going to be a wizard one day. Don't bother me with such trivialities."

Garth went white, but he faced his grandfather squarely. "I can keep her, then?"

"Oh, keep her if it means so much to you. Just keep her out of my sight. And I suggest you teach her some manners." He stalked to the study. The door snapped shut behind him.

Garth gathered Cat in trembling hands and fled to his room. Once there, he let her go and slid to the floor, leaning against the door. He stared at her.

"I don't understand."

There was no answer to that. Even if she could have spoken, what could she have said? That his grandfather was involved in a conspiracy? That he was a traitor? A traitor, like her father.

Garth shook his head. "It doesn't make sense. I thought

you wanted to be transformed, but... You did want me to keep quiet just now, didn't you?"

She nodded.

He sighed and rubbed his face. "So what do we do now?"

It was, she thought, a good question. A very good question.

Unfortunately, she had no answer.

# GAYLAND

CAT SLEPT ON THE FOOT OF GARTH'S BED that night. It was much softer than the kitchen floor, but her sleep was fitful at best. Whenever she did doze, pictures jerked her awake: pictures of black boots on the other side of the curtain, pictures of the curtain swept aside, leaving her exposed, pictures of Master Wishbe's face as he spoke of betrayal, pictures of her father's face, gazing after the man who'd just given him five gold pieces.

She must have slept at last, for she awoke abruptly when Garth sat up in bed the next morning. Wrapping his arms around his knees, he regarded her gravely.

"Have you changed your mind? Do you want me to tell Grandfather?"

Alarmed, Cat sat up and shook her head vehemently.

Garth sighed. "I don't understand, but... What about some other wizard? I don't know how many know the transformation spell, but Master Wishbe would, I'm sure, and

Master Clark. He's a good wizard and a great friend of Grandfather's. You turned down my offer of money for a finding spell, but this is different."

Cat shuddered at the very thought of going to Master Wishbe. As for Master Clark...he might be safe. But any friend of Konrad Spellman's was suspect. She shook her head again.

"Do you want to stay a cat? Is that it?" Garth sounded exasperated.

Another shake of the head.

"You shake your head at everything I suggest. What do you want me to do?"

She didn't know. She stared miserably at him.

Garth's shoulders slumped, as though the weight of the world rested heavily on them. Rising, he went over to the basin and splashed water onto his face, then took fresh clothes from his wardrobe and started to strip off his night robe.

He stopped abruptly. "I forgot you weren't really a cat," he mumbled. Even the back of his neck was red.

She jumped off the bed, walked over to the window, tail stiff, and leapt onto the window ledge. Gazing out at the garden, fresh in the early morning sunlight, she felt hot all over. She had forgotten too. Or, rather, she had and she hadn't. The curiosity she'd felt as he'd begun to strip had not been a cat's curiosity.

Garth cleared his throat noisily. She ignored him. "You'd best stay here or in the kitchen to keep out of Grandfather's way," he said. She listened to his footsteps clatter down the stairs.

It was some time before she followed him.

The day stretched before her, with only her thoughts for company. They weren't pleasant companions.

Would she ever be a girl again?

What would happen to her if Master Spellman and Master Wishbe discovered that a girl, not a cat, had overheard their plot?

What would happen to her father after he sang his song?

What would happen to Freya? Would there really be a war?

She stirred uneasily. She'd never known war. Oh, she'd heard heroic songs and stories about the Uglik War, fought over five centuries ago, when Uglessians invaded Freya only to be driven back by Freyan wizards. But Lianna had always said the tales were false, that war was cruel and ugly.

If this conspiracy might lead to war, shouldn't she stop it?

How? She couldn't talk. Even if she could, she didn't dare. Her words would send her father to prison. Or the gallows.

She prowled. She prowled in the kitchen until she was thrown out. Then she prowled in the garden.

The day dragged on, relentlessly hot. She eyed the shade under the apple tree, but was too restless to seek its shelter.

If she could persuade her father not to sing, the plot would fail. But how could she do that? She couldn't even speak to him until a wizard changed her into a girl. And she didn't dare ask a wizard to do that as long as the conspiracy existed. It was a vicious circle, going round and round, leading nowhere.

The air was still and heavy, the birds and insects silent.

Suddenly, Cat turned and streaked towards the back wall. It might do no good to seek out her father, but it was better than pacing the garden.

The streets were crammed as usual, but the pace was sluggish. Cat wove her way in and out of legs, keeping to the shade as much as possible.

It was close to the dinner hour by the time she turned the corner onto Threadmore Street, but the smell of frying fish that came from a street stall made her feel nauseated, not hungry. The face of the man frying the fish ran with sweat. He looked as hot and limp as Cat felt, as dispirited as the houses around him. Cat wondered why she'd come.

Then she saw Gayland's house. The blue door was ajar. Heart beating fast, she slipped inside.

The hall was dim, and smelled of dust. Four doors faced it, and an iron stairway led to more doors on other levels. Which one was her father's? She had no idea.

She'd come too far to turn back now. She padded from door to door, listening, sniffing. Up the stairs. More doors. Listen. Sniff.

On the top floor, she heard music. A lute, each note pure, clear, like drops of water from the brook at home. Then a voice joined the lute's melody.

But it was a woman's voice. Cat halted.

The voice broke into a deep, rasping cough that went on and on. The lute stopped. Cat crept closer.

"Oh, Lucia," a voice murmured. A man's voice. A voice she knew.

"I'll...be all...right," a woman gasped. A fresh fit of coughing seized her.

Cat heard someone move inside, then Gayland's voice. "We're out of water. I'll fetch some more."

The door opened in her face. She jumped back.

Gayland blinked. "My friend from the other night, if I'm not mistaken. What did you do, follow me home? And now you've come seeking supper. We should be able to spare you something." He waved a gallant hand, inviting her in. "Lucia, here's a friend of mine looking for a bite to eat. Can you find something while I fetch the water?"

"Of course." A dark-haired woman smiled at Cat, then coughed again. A shadow crossed Gayland's face. He hesitated, then left, closing the door quietly behind him. A moment later, Cat heard quick, light steps running down the stairs.

So this was Lucia, and she and Gayland were living together. She was beautiful, Cat admitted, with masses of dark curls and large, luminous brown eyes. But her eyes were almost too bright, there were hectic patches of red on her cheeks, and she was thin, too thin, as the minstrel in The Laughing Lute had said. Slowly, she walked over to a small chest and took out a string of sausage. She cut it into bite-sized portions and put a full plate in front of Cat.

"There." She stroked Cat's back.

Cat suffered the petting without protest. She wanted to dislike the woman, but couldn't. Lucia's voice was too kind, her touch too gentle. And she was too sick.

Gayland was back in a few minutes, bearing a jug of

water. He poured a glass and handed it to Lucia. She smiled her thanks, but made a face after her first sip.

"I don't like the taste of the water."

"It's safe enough. It's like a lot here – not the best, but it will do until we can afford better."

"Gayland, must we stay? Can't we leave Freyfall?"

"The competition –"

"I know the competition means a lot to you, but –"

"It will make our fortune."

"How can you say that? You know the successful musicians will win renown but only a token purse. Are you hoping the queen will be so impressed she'll hire you as a court musician? You'd hate living in Freybourg. So would I."

"I know. No. We'll soon settle down, but not in Freybourg. In a pretty village, in a house with a green, sunlit garden just for you."

"And you'd be content to stay there?" Skepticism filled Lucia's voice, but her mouth tilted into a smile.

"Oh, I'll wander off now and then, but I'll always come back. And when you're well enough, you can join me on the road some of the time."

"I'd like that." Her smile faded. "But Gayland, you know it's just a dream."

"Trust me. I'll get the money to buy you your garden." He turned away. Lucia looked at his averted face and sighed.

Cat glanced around. She didn't blame Lucia for wanting to leave this place. The room held a bed, a chair, a table, a chest, and two lutes leaning against the wall. That was all, but it seemed crammed. The straw mats that dotted the floor couldn't hide ancient grime any more than the smell of fresh soap could hide the rancid odour of ancient grease. Despite the open dormer window, heat clutched the room like a closed fist.

"Why don't you sing me the song you'll use in the competition?" Lucia suggested.

Gayland frowned. "It's not finished yet."

"So? I can help you with it."

"All right," Gayland agreed, a trifle reluctantly, Cat thought. "But first you must take your medicine."

Lucia made another face. "It tastes foul."

"'The worse the taste, the faster the cure,'" Gayland said, quoting an old proverb. He uncorked a bottle and poured dark, syrupy liquid into a spoon. "Open wide."

"The worse the taste, the more the cost, you mean," Lucia muttered, but she opened her mouth obediently.

Gayland recorked the bottle. "I'm sure it's helping you," he said stoutly.

Lucia said nothing. Her head was bowed, but Cat thought she caught a glint of tears.

"Now for the song," Gayland said. "And what an audience I have – my wife, the lovely and talented Lucia, and a feline of unknown origin but undoubted elegance and taste." He made them a sweeping bow.

So they were married, her father and Lucia. Well, it was to be expected, wasn't it? It didn't change anything. Why should she mind?

But she did mind, so much so that she missed the opening bars of the lute. But her attention was caught by the joyous, lilting notes that followed. The tune laughed and swirled, skipped and played, like sunlight on water. Gayland's voice took up the melody.

*I sing in the morning and I sing at noon*
*I sing in the evening at the rising of the moon*
*I sing with delight where Frey glides through the land*
*Green Freya's blessed by Freyn's loving hand.*

The lute sang along for a few notes, echoing and embellishing the refrain. Then Gayland swept into the first verse. Cat felt as though she were back on the boat sailing down the river, past farms and meadows, towns and forests. Only now she was invited to sit by the hearth in some of those farmhouses, share a flask of ale as she walked down a forest path.

Then the music slowed, hushed, sang with the purity of starlight, the serenity of sleep. Under it, like an underground spring, strains of "Sleep, My Little One" echoed and re-echoed. Cat's eyes misted, remembering her mother singing the lullaby, night after night, as she combed Cat's hair.

*And when evening ends and night's shadows fall*
*Freyn keeps His watch over one and all.*
*He guards the slumbers till the morning bell*
*Of all those in Freya, that He loves so well.*

The lute played on, soft, full of peace. Then it gradually quickened, as though stirred to new life by the first rays of dawn. The gay notes of a dance wove through the room again, but this time they seemed subtly altered by the rhythm of the sea.

*I sing in the morning and I sing at noon*
*I sing in the evening at the rising of the moon*
*I sing with delight where sea touches land*
*Blue Islandia's blessed by the Mother's loving hand.*

Cat had never seen the ocean, but she could almost smell the salt in the air, feel the sand beneath her feet and cool mist on her face, see waves curl into white foam on the shore, as Gayland sang of Islandia. Then it was the gentle, haunting lullaby again, only this time with the Mother watching over all those on Islandia.

Again the dance motif, now demanding a faster pace, greater leaps.

*I sing in the morning and I sing at noon*
*I sing in the evening at the rising of the moon*
*I sing with delight where ursells roam –*

Cat meowed. Loudly.

The music came to a jangling halt. Gayland looked at her, annoyed. "What was that all about?"

Lucia laughed and clapped her hands. "The cat's a music critic."

"If you mean I played a jarring note –"

"The notes were fine. It's the words that were wrong."

"What?"

"Ursells are such undignified beasts. They don't belong in your song. The cat knows." She laughed again.

"A cat that understands Freyan." Gayland snorted, but he looked uncomfortable. Cat was glad. She meowed even louder.

"You see? The cat says you can't use ursells."

Gayland chuckled. "A cat with strong opinions." He rose.

"No, go on."

"It's not finished. A good place to end for now. I have to work on the rest."

"What you have so far is beautiful," Lucia said softly. Pride shone in her eyes. "You're sure to be chosen."

"Thank you, kind lady." Gayland bowed grandly. "And what does my other critic think?" He glanced at Cat, smiling.

Cat agreed. With a cold fear that sat like lead in her stomach, she too thought the song was sure to be chosen.

"You may laugh, but did you see how attentively she listened?" Lucia asked.

Gayland grinned. "A musical cat like this one belongs in the family. What do you say we keep her?"

"It would be nice to have another member of the family," Lucia said wistfully. "And she could chase the mice away too. I hear them scratching behind the walls sometimes, especially at night when I can't sleep."

The grin faded from Gayland's face, but he said heartily, "So be it, then. We'll adopt her if she'll have us. What do you say, cat?"

Wasn't this what she wanted? What she had come to Freyfall for? To be with her father? Not as a cat, preferably. But still...if she were here, perhaps she could stop him.

How? Meow every time he used the word "ursell"?

No. She needed help. Human help. Garth's help.

Garth. He'd be worried about her. She glanced at the window to gauge the time, but the sun was hidden by a dense mass of black clouds.

She must get home. She walked to the door and meowed.

Gayland looked surprised. "You want to go?"

She scratched at the wood.

"Very well. If you say so." He opened the door.

"Even a stray cat doesn't want to stay here." Lucia gave a bitter laugh that turned into a jagged cough. Cat gave a last look over her shoulder as she left. Lucia huddled in the chair, racked by coughs.

Cat raced down the stairs and out the door just before a large, red-faced woman closed it.

It was cooler now. Dark was rolling in with the clouds. People hurried to get indoors. Cat trotted down the street, instinctively heading for the Spellmans', but her thoughts were in the tiny room she'd just left.

He was a good man, her father. Kind. Generous. A fine musician. He had joined the conspiracy because he needed money. Money for Lucia.

If she could get help for Lucia, Gayland wouldn't need the money. He wouldn't sing his song.

Could Garth find her a healer? But healers were expensive.

A man jogged past her, heading for shelter.

Could she find a way to ask Garth to lend her the money?

No! Even if Garth had enough to pay for a healer's services, it wasn't right. He had already bought her flute. Where was her pride? Her sense of fairness? Was Garth supposed to pay and pay and pay for his one mistake?

*I can't afford to be proud. I can't afford to be fair.*

Then the skies opened and rain pelted down. Cat forgot everything else and dashed for the refuge of a recessed doorway.

# A Night of Music

I T HAD BEEN DARK FOR SEVERAL HOURS BY THE time Cat dragged her wet, weary, and bedraggled body back to 6 Gotham Street. She sat in the garden and looked at the shadowy house. The rain had stopped, and a few stars glittered coldly in the night sky. They were the only lights she could see.

No. A glimmer of light flickered in an upstairs room. Was it...? She peered upwards. Yes. It was Garth's room. She let out the loudest meow she could utter. A head appeared in the window, then disappeared. A few minutes later, the back door opened. Candle in hand, Garth looked out.

"Cat? Is that you, cat?"

With a sigh of relief, Cat trotted towards him.

"Where have you been? I've been so worried. Why, you're soaked."

Cat proved his words by shaking herself and showering him. Garth wiped his face. "I suppose I'd better carry you, or you'll get dirty paw prints all over the house."

All this had been said in a whisper. Garth blew out his candle and picked Cat up. As they progressed through the lightless hall and up the stairs, Cat wished she could lend Garth her night sight. At one point, he bumped into a table and cursed under his breath.

In his room, the boy let her go, relit his candle, then sat down on the edge of his bed. With a twinge of guilt, Cat noticed that the front of his nightshirt was smudged. She set about cleaning herself.

"Where were you?" Garth repeated. He sighed. "Oh, I know you can't answer. I wish you could talk. Or even write."

Cat raised her head abruptly. Talk. Write. She could do neither. But maybe she could speak to him. In a way.

Looking around, she spied a book lying open on the nightstand. She leapt onto the table and scanned the page.

"What are you doing?"

She spotted a word and pointed to it.

"What? Oh. You're pointing to words. Words that will tell me something. Is that it?"

She meowed.

"What a good idea." He bent over the book. "Went... Yes. Went where?"

The word father did not appear on the open pages. Frustrated, Cat pawed at the book, trying to turn the pages.

"Wait. I've got an idea." Hastily, Garth opened a drawer in the nightstand and dug out a blank sheet of paper, an inkwell, and a pen. "I'll write out the letters of the alphabet."

It was slow, but it worked.

"Father. You went to see your father?"

She pointed to other letters.

"You...go...see...him. Me? You want me to see your father? Do you want me to tell him who you are?"

Cat considered this. Would Gayland change his plan, knowing she had overheard his conversation with Master Wishbe? She doubted it. She shook her head.

"No? Then why...? Never mind. I'll go with you to see him. I owe you that." He yawned. "It's awfully late. Why don't we both go to sleep?"


MASTER SPELLMAN kept Garth occupied most of the next day. It wasn't until late afternoon, when the wizard left the house, that Garth was free to collect Cat and leave. He sought out his mother first.

"I'm going out. Don't worry if I'm late getting home."

Annette Spellman's welcoming smile faded. "But Garth, it's close to dinnertime."

"I'll grab something from the kitchen before I go."

"But your grandfather's just come back."

"So? He's gone out too."

"He'll be home for dinner, and he'll expect to see you there."

"All he does is bark questions at me and sneer at my answers. Dinner will be more comfortable without me." There was a hard edge in Garth's voice that Cat hadn't heard before.

Mistress Spellman frowned. "Your grandfather cares about you, Garth."

"Cares? All he cares about is that I become a good wizard and don't disgrace the Spellman name."

"That's not true, Garth."

"Isn't it? If he really cared, he'd let me play music. It's all I want, all I dream of." His voice shook.

"Garth... It's just that Spellmans have been wizards for generations and generations. I know how you feel, but... He was so hurt when Wendell died."

"Oh, Father was a perfect son, I know. And a perfect wizard. He would have made Grandfather a wonderful heir. But I'm not Father. I don't have his talent."

"You could be a good wizard if you tried."

"I do try. I just can't do it."

"You try – up to a point. Then your mind wanders."

Garth was silent.

"Please stay for dinner," Mistress Spellman said softly.

"I'm sorry. I have to go out."

His mother's lips tightened. "Very well."

"Mother, I'm sorry. I know it's hard on you, having to tell Grandfather I'm gone. But –"

"Go." Mistress Spellman walked away. Garth watched her retreating back.

Cat did too. This was her fault. All her fault.

No, it wasn't. If Garth's mind hadn't wandered, if he hadn't turned her into a cat, she wouldn't need him now.

All the long way to Threadmore Street, while Garth strode along, glancing neither left nor right, Cat revolved various plans in her head. None worked. Her only hope lay in Garth's ability to help Lucia.

It was cooler than it had been yesterday, but again the faded blue door was propped open to catch the breeze. Once inside, Cat jumped down from Garth's shoulders and led the way to her father's room. Garth hesitated, glanced at her, then tapped lightly.

Lucia opened the door. "Yes?"

"I...I'm sorry," Garth stammered. "I'm looking for someone else. A man named Gayland Bellmore."

"My husband's out at the moment, but —" her eyes fell on Cat. "Why, if it's not our friend the musical cat, back with a new friend. Come in."

Cat entered. Garth followed, looking uncomfortable.

"Please sit down."

Garth glanced at the sole chair, and remained standing. His eyes roved around the shabby room, then came to rest on the lutes leaning against the wall. Lucia followed his gaze.

"Are you a musician too?"

"Yes. That is...no. Not really."

Lucia's eyebrows lifted.

"I like to play, but I don't have much time. I'm apprenticed to a different trade."

"But you are a music lover. I knew the cat would bring someone musical." She laughed in delight, then grabbed the chair back as a spasm of coughing shook her. Garth watched her in alarm, then took her arm gently and helped her into the chair. Hacking coughs shuddered through her thin body.

"Can I get you anything? Medicine...?"

"Had it," Lucia gasped, nodding at the bottle on the windowsill. She fumbled in her pocket and came out with a handkerchief, which she held to her mouth. Finally the wrenching cough subsided. Lucia straightened and returned the handkerchief to her pocket. Cat noticed a smear of red on it.

"Sorry. These spells catch me suddenly."

"Have you seen a healer?"

She nodded. "Yes, a Master Birchill. He sold us the medicine and told me to get plenty of food and rest." She grimaced. "A fine thing to tell a wandering musician."

Garth frowned. "Surely –"

"Oh, I'm taking it easy. Gayland makes sure of that." She smiled. "He even talks about settling down in a quiet town and buying a small house with a sunny garden." Her smile faded. "It's a pretty dream."

Footsteps could be heard, leaping lightly up the stairs. Lucia's face brightened. A moment later, the door opened and Cat's father walked in.

"Look who's returned," Lucia greeted him. "The musical cat, and brought a musical friend with her."

"How pleasant," Gayland said. "Any friend of this cat's a friend of ours, and a music lover is doubly welcome." His tone was light, but Cat noted the worry in his eyes as they examined Lucia's face. He knelt to stroke Cat. "Does she belong to you?"

"She's...staying with me for a time," Garth said, choosing his words with care.

Gayland laughed. "An independent puss. And did she really lead you here?"

"Yes."

"We'll have to find a bowl of milk for her. And I'm sure we have food for a guest." He looked enquiringly at Lucia.

Garth flushed. "We've just eaten, both of us. We didn't come –"

"They've come for music, of course," Lucia interrupted, eyes sparkling. "A feast of music awaits us."

A feast it was. Cat sat on the floor and listened as the others played and sang. She just wished she could join in. Once she forgot herself and opened her mouth, producing a yowl so awful it brought tears of laughter to all their eyes.

Garth's initial shyness melted. Borrowing Gayland's lute, he even played a few of his own compositions. Cat was surprised at how good they were, and Gayland and Lucia heaped high praise on him. Colour flooded his face. Eyes shining, he listened to Lucia's and Gayland's songs, and joined Lucia with entreaties that Gayland share the piece he'd written about the three lands.

"I won't be entering the competition, so there's no fear I'll steal it," he pointed out.

Gayland shook his head. "It's not that. It's just that I don't feel good about it."

"But it's a beautiful song," Lucia protested.

Gayland shook his head again, and swung into a song so funny that his audience forgot everything else and howled with laughter.

It was a magical evening, an evening to cradle in one's mind like a beloved child. It was marred only by Lucia's frequent fits of coughing. Gayland's eyes were fixed on her face at such times. So, Cat noticed, were Garth's.

It wasn't until a beam of moonlight rested on the lute in Gayland's hand that Garth jumped to his feet.

"It's late. I must be off. Thank you. Thank you so much."

Gayland rose from the bed where they'd both been sitting. "It was our pleasure."

"Please come again," Lucia urged. "You and the cat. What's her name, by the way? And yours?" She picked Cat up and held her. She smelled of fragrant soap, but underneath that, Cat smelled something else. Something sour. A whiff of blood. A whiff of bile.

"My name's Garth. I just call the cat 'cat.'"

Lucia smiled. "It suits her. Will you come again?"

"I'd love to. Is there any time that's inconvenient for you?"

"I'll be out three nights from now," Gayland said. "Some people to see," he added shortly as Lucia looked at him with surprise.

Cat's breath caught. Of course. His meeting with Master Wishbe.

"Any other evening, then," Lucia told Garth.

"Thank you. It's been a wonderful night."

"And for us," Lucia said. She stroked Cat, her hand loving. Cat felt a purr rumble inside her.

"Indeed," Gayland agreed. "It's a gift having a young person around."

*You could have had me around all these years,* Cat thought. The purr died stillborn.

Garth walked briskly through the dark streets, but Cat

heard the chimes strike one as they reached 6 Gotham Street. Garth fumbled with his key, but before he could unlock the door, it opened in his face.

"Welcome home," Master Spellman said.

Garth returned the key to his pocket. Cat felt his body go tense.

"I'm sorry I'm late," he muttered.

"Late? You think it's late? But it's only one in the morning, the time any young man would be coming home, surely."

Garth said nothing.

"And may I enquire what kept you?" Master Spellman asked politely, stepping back to let Garth enter. A low candle guttered on a small table by the stairs, casting cavernous shadows on the wizard's face.

"I...met some people."

"Oh? And might these...people...be musicians, by any chance?"

"Yes, but –"

"Yes? Why am I not surprised somehow?"

"Grandfather, I had a good reason. I –"

"My grandson and apprentice goes out without his dinner on my third night home, stays out till one in the morning, neglecting his work and worrying his mother sick, but he has a reason. It's for his music, of course." Konrad Spellman's voice was soft, but it cut like a whip.

Cat cringed. She wished she could disappear into the darkness beyond the candle's glow. Without meaning to, she dug her claws into Garth's shoulder. She withdrew them immediately, but she doubted that Garth even noticed. He was trembling, but when he spoke his voice was steady.

"Where is Mother?"

"In bed. I managed to convince her, finally, that you were neither lost, strayed, nor stolen, but merely...occupied, shall we say? I suggest you go to bed too. Your work begins early in the morning, whether you like it or not."

Without a word, Garth walked past his grandfather and up the stairs to his room. Once there, Cat jumped to the floor and watched as Garth picked up the nearest object and hurled it across the room. It was a heavy pitcher of water, and it struck the wall with a crack that shattered it into jagged shards. Water ran down the wall and across the floor.

Garth looked around wildly for something else to throw. Cat meowed loudly. He looked at her, and some of the fury drained from his face.

"Freyn curse him, he makes me so furious sometimes..." He stood a moment, the tension gradually easing from his body. His shoulders slumped. "I'm sorry, Cat. I didn't mean to alarm you."

Slowly, he walked over to the shattered remains of the pitcher. Cat wished she could help, but all she could do was watch as he picked up the biggest pieces and used his boot to brush the fragments into a corner.

"There. That will have to do till morning. Won't Mistress Fairway be angry when she finds them." He sighed and sat on the bed. He looked at Cat.

"I suppose it seems silly to you to be worried about a broken jug, or even about what Grandfather thinks of me."

She didn't think it was silly at all. She shook her head.

A small smile flickered across Garth's face, then disappeared. He stared at nothing for a long moment, then said softly, almost to himself, "I sometimes think I hate him."

He fell silent. Cat waited, but he said nothing more. She curled up on a small rug, out of the way of the water.

Finally, Garth shook himself and looked at her again. "Did you take me there tonight to see if I could help Lucia?"

Her ears pricked. She sat up.

"Well, I can't. I'm sorry."

She stared at him.

"Don't look at me like that. I'm sorry, but...I don't know very much about healing. Even if I were a good wizard, I probably wouldn't. Few wizards do, unless they specialize in healing magic, and even then... Well, I sometimes think they don't know much either."

She couldn't believe it. She wouldn't believe it. Wizards could do impossible things. Even transform girls into cats and transform them back. At least, she prayed that they could.

As though reading her mind, Garth said, "I know it seems strange, when we can do so much, that we're not very good at curing illness." He paused, then said thoughtfully, "I've heard that some wizards have learned ways of healing from the wise women of Islandia, who are so much better at it than we are." He took a deep breath, then let it out slowly. "I'll ask Grandfather if he knows any. But this healer of Lucia's is probably right. Rest and good food are the best medicines."

The hope he offered was as feeble as a dying child. Cat stared into a black future as Garth snuffed out his candle and crawled into bed.

Gayland would sing his song. Then what? What would happen to him? What would happen to Freya? War?

Clouds must have blown in. There was no glimmer of moonlight or starshine. The darkness in the room was so dense Cat felt she could touch it. It seemed to creep into her own mind, her own heart.

"Cat?" Garth's voice was muffled, though he didn't seem to be talking into his pillow. She jumped onto the bed and padded towards him. His hand reached out, touched her, stroked her. She settled down beside him. His hand continued to move, slowly, lovingly. Finally, they both slept.

# A Plotting of Conspirators

ALL THE NEXT DAY, THE SUN BEAT DOWN ON a baking city. It did nothing, however, to thaw the ice fog that wrapped the Spellman household.

Cat crept past the closed study door a few times, but heard nothing. She pictured Garth and his grandfather sitting in frigid silence, and winced. Slipping into the kitchen, she ate her food hastily. Even Mistress Grove's usual cheer was muted, whether by Master Spellman's mood or by Mistress Fairway's tight-lipped fury over the smashed pitcher, Cat didn't know. She fled to the safety of the garden and lay under the apple tree, brooding.

What should she do about the conspiracy and her father's role in it? What *could* she do?

Gayland was to meet Master Wishbe two nights from now. Should she go to The Merry Jug, listen to their plans? Should she take Garth with her?

But what if Garth went to the authorities with news of

the plot? Gayland would be in trouble. Big trouble.

Garth wouldn't do that, surely. After all, his grandfather was one of the conspirators.

Would he care? He had said he sometimes thought he hated his grandfather.

Perhaps she should do nothing.

But then she would be responsible. If war came, it would be her fault.

If only her mother were here. Lianna would know what to do.

In mid-afternoon, Annette Spellman came to the garden and sat beside Cat. She said nothing, but stroked the cat gently. Some of the strain left her face as Cat snuggled closer.

That night, Garth was as quenched as the candle he blew out before getting into bed. He was silent for some time, though Cat sensed he wasn't asleep.

"I didn't ask Grandfather about healers today. I meant to, but... I'm sorry. I will tomorrow."

But he didn't. Cat understood his reluctance, but it frustrated her. The next morning, she crept into the study early and hid behind the curtains. When Konrad Spellman's back was turned, she'd make sure Garth saw her and remembered his promise.

She didn't have to. No sooner had Master Spellman curtly informed his apprentice about his allotted activities than Garth cleared his throat.

"Grandfather..."

"What? I thought my instructions were clear."

"Yes. Of course. It wasn't... I was wondering –"

"What? How to get out of your work?"

"No!" Garth sounded angry. Perhaps his anger helped. He continued in a firmer tone, "Are there any Islandian-trained healers in Freya?"

There was a pause. Then his grandfather asked, "Why?"

"Why? Well, I just... They're the best healers, aren't they?"

"Undoubtedly. I was simply surprised by your interest. It's a rare day indeed when you volunteer a question about any matter related to wizardry." Master Spellman's voice was caustic. If Cat had been in Garth's shoes, she would have been tempted to stalk out of the room, slamming the door behind her. Luckily, Garth did no such thing.

"Are there?" he persisted. "Any Islandian-style healers?"

"To be a true Islandian healer, you have to be born with the gift – a rarity in Islandia, and unknown in Freya. As for Freyans trained in Islandian healing ways – there's Kerstin Brooks, of course, and I think she's taught a couple of promising apprentices the methods. I don't know where they are now. Somewhere in the Frey-by-the-Sea area, I imagine. Mistress Glenbrook at the College learned a bit. She's dead now, but she may have passed on some knowledge to our current crop of healers. If so, they've shown few signs of that knowledge." Master Spellman snorted, then continued, "One of the goals of the upcoming gathering of wizards is to persuade Islandians to spend a couple of years teaching at the College."

"But you don't know anyone living in Freyfall or close by who is trained now?"

"No. Now stop wasting time and return to your work," Master Spellman said, but his voice was less harsh than it had been.

Cat contemplated the information as the morning inched on. There was nothing else to contemplate except the crimson curtains in front of her, the polished floor beneath her, and the scratch of quill pens in the room beyond.

So there were few good healers in Freya, and none in Freyfall. There might be in the future, but that did her no good. And there might not be, if the conspirators had their way and the Uglessians and Islandians left Freya in disgust.

She must make sure they didn't.

She needed Garth's help.

Cat remained hidden for what seemed more like a week than a day, not even leaving when Garth and his grandfather departed for their noon meal. Twice, visitors arrived, seeking the wizard's help.

In late afternoon, a light knock came at the study door. "Come in," Master Spellman barked.

Cat heard Mistress Fairway's voice. "I'm sorry to disturb you, sir, but a messenger's just arrived with a note for you. He's waiting for a reply."

Paper rustled. Konrad Spellman exclaimed, "Jem! He's in town early. Tell the messenger to say that of course I'll come to dinner with him. In fact, I'll go right now. No, wait. There's that meeting tonight. Never mind. I'll let them know I can't make it."

His pen scratched. A moment later, Cat heard him stride from the room. She crept out.

"Cat! Have you been here all along? I wondered where you were when I couldn't find you at noon. Did you hear what Grandfather said about healers?"

Ignoring his question, Cat jumped onto the desk and pointed to the book lying open in front of him.

"What? Oh, you want to tell me something, do you? Wait a minute." He grabbed a sheet of paper and scribbled out the alphabet. "Go ahead."

Cat pointed to the letters she needed.

"Go...tavern...Merry...Jug." He looked at her. "You want us to go to this tavern, wherever it is? I've never heard of it. Cat...I don't know. I'm in deep enough disgrace already. Why should I go there? What's at this tavern?"

What would he say if she spelled out "a plotting of conspirators?" Would he even believe her? She pointed to the letters for "important."

Garth sighed. "All right. If you say so. I suppose I can't be in much more trouble than I'm in now. Grandfather's always disappointed in me no matter what I do. Anyway, he's out tonight himself. Still, I don't want to worry Mother about having to decide whether or not to let me leave. We'll have to sneak out. When do we go?"

The meeting was unlikely to take place till after dark, Cat thought. But she had no idea how long it would take to find The Merry Jug. She pointed "after dinner."

They slipped out the back door shortly after they'd eaten. Garth had told his mother he'd be in his room all evening. She'd asked no questions.

Finding The Merry Jug proved no easy task. Passersby

shook their heads at Garth's question, or gave vague, uncertain directions. The long, slow midsummer evening had faded into dusk by the time they finally located it, on a dingy street on Freyfall's central island. Merry it was not, Cat decided, surveying the low building with its sagging roof.

Garth eyed it dubiously. "Is this really where you want to go?"

Cat made a noise she hoped he'd recognize as assent.

"Hmm. I wish I knew why. Well..." He headed towards the door.

Cat meowed loudly and dug her claws into his shoulder.

He stopped. "We're not to go in. Is that it? Then what are we doing here?"

Now that they'd arrived, Cat wasn't sure. She could slip inside and hide in some dark corner, but what about Garth?

She looked around. There. A narrow gap lay between the tavern and the adjacent building. She jumped down and led the way, first checking to make sure no one was watching.

If Garth had been any wider, he would have had to edge in sideways. The gap was small, and dark, and smelled as though garbage had been thrown in it for years and left to rot.

"Cat, what in Freyn's name –"

Cat hissed. The window above them was open to catch the evening air. It would make it easy for them to hear conversations inside. It also made it easy for those inside to hear them.

Garth dropped his voice to a low mutter. "Do we have to stay here?"

Cat made a small assenting noise. Garth grunted, then leaned against the wall behind him and folded his arms across his chest, gazing steadily and, Cat thought, accusingly, at her. She didn't blame him. She wouldn't have blamed him if he'd turned on his heel and walked away. But he didn't.

They waited. Waited as the dusk deepened into night and a thin sliver of moon appeared. Waited as the late revellers left the tavern and staggered down the road. The stench seemed to worsen. Rustling, gnawing noises signalled the presence of rodents. Cat's ears pricked. Her body stretched into a hunter's pose. She forced her muscles to relax.

Finally, their patience was rewarded. A man, hooded and cloaked despite the warmth of the summer night, walked up the street and entered The Merry Jug. Cat caught her breath as she heard him settle in a chair right above them.

"A bottle of wine and two glasses, Casper," he called.

"Someone joining you then?"

"Yes. First one man. After he goes, two more."

Cat heard Garth suck in his breath. He, too, must have recognized the voice. Master Wishbe.

A few minutes later, another figure approached the tavern. But this one sauntered, whistling, hands in pockets, bare head raised to view the stars. Gayland Bellmore looked like the last person in the world to be involved in a conspiracy.

He went in. Cat heard his voice above her head.

"Freyn's night to you."

"Keep your voice down," Master Wishbe hissed.

Gayland laughed. "Why? We're the only ones here besides the tavern keeper, who I presume is in on this." Nevertheless, he spoke more softly. Cat had to strain to hear him. Beside her, she felt Garth lean forward.

"Are the songs ready?" Master Wishbe demanded.

"Aside from some polishing."

"Will they do?"

"Who can say? I think they're good, but then I'm biased."

"Let me hear them."

"You want me to sing to you?" Gayland sounded amused.

"Don't be a fool. Of course not. Just tell me the words."

"This is the one I'll sing for the judges."

Once again, Cat heard Gayland evoke the three lands: green Freya, wave-kissed Islandia, rock-bound Uglessia. Once again, she heard him waken echoes of a beloved lullaby as he spoke of the love and care given by Freyn, the Mother, and the spirits. Then he went on, conjured up a vision where the beauty and strength of three lands and peoples were united.

"And the other song?" Master Wishbe asked impatiently as soon as the first one had ended. "The one you'll actually sing?"

"It's identical except for the last three verses. I thought you might appreciate that, since you want to infer that the queen's musicians – and by implication the queen herself – are in on the jest."

He recited.

*And when evening ends and night's shadows fall*
*The spirits keep their watch over one and all*
*They guard the slumbers, but find it hard to tell*
*Which dreams come from people, which from ursells.*

*And now we are joining our minds and our hearts*
*And here we are sharing in our magic arts:*
*The knowledge of Freya, the wisdom of the west*
*The instincts of the beast, by the spirits blessed.*

*For which is man, which beast, when dressed in ursell grey?*
*And who can tell the difference in what they do and say?*
*So here's to our union of mind and heart and — smell*
*Let's sing on our way till the tolling of the bell.*

Silence followed his final words. Then Master Wishbe asked, "Tolling of the bell?"

"The death toll, made obvious by the notes I will play on the lute."

"I see." Another, briefer silence. "It will do. Here's your pay." Cat heard the thud of a purse landing on the table, then the clink of coins being taken out and counted.

"Are you satisfied?" Master Wishbe asked sarcastically.

"No."

"What do you mean? It's all there."

"I want all my pay now."

"Now? But we agreed —"

"I've been thinking, and I don't much like my thoughts. The money won't do me much good if I'm locked in prison."

"I've told you –"

"That you'll look after me. Quite. Pardon me if I seem to doubt your word, but I want all my pay now."

"You'll take the money and run."

"No."

The wizard snorted.

Gayland said persuasively, "Give me the money after my song has been chosen by the judges. I swear in Freyn's name I'll show up to sing at the council."

A pause. Then Master Wishbe said, "Half the final sum after you're chosen. The rest after you've sung."

"Agreed."

Chair legs scraped back. Gayland said, "Shall we meet here, at the same time, after the competition results are known?"

"Very well."

"Farewell, then, till I see you again – with my money."

A moment later, Cat saw her father emerge into the night and stroll back down the street. Garth stirred, but Cat stayed still. Master Wishbe had said two others would join him later. She wanted to know who they were. Garth settled back against the wall.

They didn't have long to wait. Within fifteen minutes, two hooded figures approached from different directions and entered the tavern.

"Well?" demanded a deep voice above her. "Has the musician composed his song?"

"He has."

"And will it do?"

"It will suit our purpose very well."

"Ah, good," said another voice, a soft one with a slight lisp. "So our plans are progressing nicely."

"They are indeed. Have you brought the knife?"

The knife? What was this? Cat's hair prickled.

"I have. A true Uglessian knife, and well used. It will look quite authentic."

"But surely everyone who enters will be searched for weapons," objected the deep-voiced man.

"Unfortunately, one of my men will have proved careless. I shall have to take strong disciplinary measures," the man with the lisp said. He laughed.

They were planning to use a knife. A Uglessian knife. Why?

Were they going to kill someone and blame it on the Uglessians? Who...?

Who but the musician who had insulted all Uglessians?

Cat felt sick.

Garth must have reached the same conclusion at the same moment. He gasped.

"What was that?" Master Wishbe asked sharply.

Cat tensed, ready to run. Garth looked about wildly.

But it was too late. An angry, alarmed face had appeared at the window and was staring at them.

# Caught

Cat's heart lurched, then started to pound. Unable to move or look away, she stared at the bearded face that loomed above her.

Then an arm reached out and grabbed Garth by the collar.

"What are you doing here?" growled the deep voice.

Garth said nothing. Cat, pressed against his leg, felt the tremors that shook him.

A clamour of voices, raised in alarm, came from within.

"A spy," said Garth's captor, not looking away. "Go out and bring him in, Penner."

The door opened. Quick footsteps headed towards them.

There was nothing holding her there. No outstretched arm. No suspicious eyes. No one would stop a cat streaking away, dashing for safety.

*Run!* screamed an inner voice.

Beside her, Garth was trembling.

She had led Garth here. She had led him into the heart of conspiracy, the heart of danger. She couldn't desert him.

She couldn't help him. She couldn't.

But to leave him alone...

Then the decision was taken from her. A shadow, darker than the shadowed recess, towered before them. The man's shoulders scraped the sides of the buildings.

"Well, well, a cat," said the soft, lisping voice. The man bent and scooped Cat up into his left arm. Instinctively, desperately, her claws went out. Raked his arm. He cursed and tightened his grip, then grabbed Garth with his right hand. The other man let go.

"Come along." A laugh. A soft lisp. But there was nothing gay in the cruel grip imprisoning Cat, nothing soft in the hand that dragged Garth out of his narrow hideaway.

The tavern was dimly lit. Even so, it took Cat's eyes a moment to adjust after the darkness outside. The three conspirators and the tavern owner were the only occupants, but the low-beamed, stone-walled room seemed crowded. Maybe that was because all four men were staring at them.

"So what do we have?" Master Wishbe asked, his voice high. "A spy, you said."

"He was outside the window," said the bearded man. He was surprisingly small for someone with such a deep voice. "I wonder how much he heard." Unlike Master Wishbe, his voice was calm. The calmness was more frightening, somehow. Fingers of ice ran up and down Cat's spine. Shudders racked her.

"Dangerous spies, I'd say – a boy and a cat. Did the cat

come to spy too?" said the tavern keeper from behind the bar. He cackled.

Master Wishbe shot him an irritated glance, but his voice was less agitated when he spoke again. "Bring him closer to the light, Penner."

Their captor obliged. In the brighter light, Cat saw that Garth's face was ashen, his eyes huge.

"What were you doing?" Master Wishbe began, then stopped. He leaned forward. "Why, you're Konrad Spellman's grandson!" he exclaimed.

"What's Spellman's grandson doing skulking outside the window?" demanded the deep-voiced man.

Master Wishbe looked at him, annoyed. "How should I know, Birchill? Well?" he barked at Garth. "What are you doing here? Did your grandfather tell you to come?"

Garth stared at him.

"Speak up, boy. Did Spellman send you with a message, since he couldn't make it here himself?"

Cat wouldn't have thought Garth could turn any whiter, but he did. He swayed as though hit.

This was their chance. Their only chance.

*Please, Garth, don't throw it away. Please. Please.*

If only she could talk. If only she could tell Master Wishbe that yes, his co-conspirator had sent them with a message.

She couldn't speak, but she could meow. She did so. Loudly.

It seemed to help. Garth steadied himself. Cat saw him breathe deeply. "Grandfather heard that an old friend was in town. He couldn't come to the meeting," he said carefully.

"I know that. He sent me a note," Master Wishbe said impatiently. "But he didn't say anything about you being here in his stead."

"No. He...it was a last minute decision. He wanted...that is, he wondered if there was anything he should know."

Master Wishbe snorted. "Didn't trust me to tell him everything, hey? Well, since you're here –"

"Wait," said the man holding Cat. He hadn't relaxed his grip on her at all, and she could see his fingers digging into Garth's arm. "Why was he hiding outside if Spellman sent him?"

"A good point. Well?" Master Wishbe asked Garth.

Cat's breath caught. What reason could there be? What possible reason?

Garth answered steadily. "I arrived a bit early. I didn't know how long it would take to get here. A man was ahead of me. I watched him enter the building, and... Well, Grandfather had impressed on me the need for secrecy, so I decided to wait till he'd gone. Even after he left and the others came, I waited. I wanted to make sure they were the right ones. I was just about to come in when you heard me. I'm sorry. I know I should have told you who I was and why I was here right away, but... Well, the truth is, I guess you scared me a bit." Garth gave what looked, even to Cat, like a shamefaced smile.

There was a long silence. Then Master Birchill nodded, Master Wishbe said, "All right," and the hand gripping Garth's arm let go. Cat was released at the same time. She only had a second to get her legs under her before she landed.

"Sit down," Master Wishbe told Garth, nodding to a chair beside his. Garth slumped onto the seat. Cat wondered if his legs were as wobbly as hers were.

"What did your grandfather tell you?" the wizard asked.

Garth hesitated. "Not much," he said cautiously. "There wasn't time."

Master Wishbe clucked his tongue impatiently and waited.

"He said you were planning to wreck the council and drive a wedge between Freyans and their neighbours. That's all, except that I overheard what the singer said."

"So you know about the song. You can tell Spellman that our plans in that department are progressing nicely, but that the musician is getting greedy. He demanded his whole fee before the event. I promised him half, and I think he wants the money badly enough that he'll sing for the other half. Still...he's nervous. Tell your grandfather he must attend our next meeting with the man. I've promised we'll look after him, but he may put more reliance on your grandfather. Everyone knows that Konrad Spellman keeps his word – and that he's got friends in high places. Tell your grandfather to meet us here the night the competition results are made known, and to bring fifty gold coins with him. This minstrel comes high, Freyn curse him."

Garth nodded woodenly.

"Why couldn't he come tonight?" Master Birchill demanded.

"An old friend arrived in town."

Master Birchill frowned. "I know that. But seeing an old

friend is scarcely as important as attending this meeting."

Master Wishbe smiled smugly. "It is in this case. The friend is Jem Brooks."

"Brooks! But he's a Uglessian lover. He and his wife have worked all these years to draw us closer to Uglessians – yes, and to those women in Islandia who've convinced everyone that they're so much better healers than Freyan wizards. He and his wife –"

"Are responsible for much of the growing closeness among the three lands. And for this council. That's right."

"Then why –"

"Jem Brooks probably knows just who will attend the council."

There was silence for a moment. Then the other man asked, "What do you mean?"

"Jem and Kerstin Brooks know more than any other Freyans about just which Islandians and Uglessians will be there and what their temperaments – and tempers – are like."

There was another silence. Then the tall man laughed and clapped Master Wishbe on the back. "In other words, they know just who will be most enraged by the song, who's most likely to seek revenge. And Brooks is sure to divulge such information to his old friend. Good for you, Wishbe. I must admit, I had my doubts about asking Spellman to join us. But you were right. Once I know the best target, I'll stick to him closer than butter to bread." He sounded light-hearted, almost gay.

"This isn't a game," Master Wishbe said sharply. "May I remind you, Captain Penner, that we are trying to save Freya."

"Of course. But I can still enjoy myself." The tall man laughed again and glanced at a nearby table.

Cat followed his gaze. A long, curved knife, unlike any she had seen before, lay on the table. She stared at it.

*Tempers.*

*Revenge.*

*That blade. That sharp, curving blade. Plunging into Gayland's chest. Plunging into his heart.*

Cat shut her eyes, but she couldn't shut out the picture.

"Well, boy, that's all you need to know. Just tell your grandfather what I told you."

"I'll tell him."

Cat heard Garth rise. A moment later, she was lifted in his arms. He held her tightly.

The night was quiet, the streets deserted. Only Garth's footsteps, and his jagged breathing, broke the silence. A breeze had sprung up. It ruffled Cat's fur. She huddled closer to the boy's chest, her body shuddering, but could find no warmth. No warmth anywhere.

Suddenly Garth stopped. They were in a large public square. A fountain arched and glistened, sprinkling crystal drops into the air and onto the cobblestones.

"Oh, cat, how could he? How could he? And what am I to do? Oh, what am I to do?"

Garth sank onto the street, his back against the fountain, and broke into a storm of racking, tearing sobs. He still held Cat close, but she offered no comfort. She had none to give.

# CAT & MOUSE

CAT STARED AT THE KITCHEN HEARTH, BUT she didn't see the flames or the heavy iron pot simmering above them. She saw The Merry Jug. She saw a bearded face below a heavy hood, framed by the tavern window. She saw a knife.

She had worried that Garth would inform the authorities about the plot. Now she wished he would. If Gayland were in prison, at least he wouldn't be killed.

But Garth had no intention of telling anyone. That was the one thing he had decided to do – or, rather, not do. When his sobs had finally subsided, he'd gazed in front of him for a long time, then said, "I have to stop them. But how? I can't – I *can't* – tell anyone. Not with Grandfather involved."

He looked down at Cat then. "And your father too. Oh, cat, I'm sorry."

Perhaps he didn't realize that Captain Penner planned to stick a knife into Gayland and blame it on the Uglessians. Or perhaps he did know but wouldn't act anyway.

Cat didn't know how long they'd stayed there. The crystal drops arched and fell, arched and fell. The crescent moon moved slowly through the sky, then was blotted out by clouds. Garth climbed wearily to his feet and trudged home. By the time they'd slipped through the garden and let themselves in, a thin, drizzling rain had started. In between spells of restless sleep, Cat had been conscious of the steady drumming of rain on the roof. It had continued through the morning, forcing her to stay indoors. She had taken refuge in the kitchen after being shooed out of Garth's room by Mistress Fairway.

She was tired. The kitchen was warm, the flickering flames hypnotic. Even Gayland's plight couldn't keep Cat's eyes open. She slept.

She woke suddenly. There was something. A noise. Scratching. Behind the wooden baseboard. Her ears pricked. Her nose twitched.

More scratching. Claws. Small claws on a stone floor. Behind the wall. Ahead of her, just ahead, was a hole. She lay still. Deceptively inert. Eyes open a mere slit.

There. A nose appeared. Whiskers. A triangular face. Sharp eyes peered at Cat. Her eyelids drooped.

Cautiously, eyes fixed on Cat, the rest of the small, grey body emerged. Four legs. A long, whiplike tail.

The mouse moved. Cat's foreleg flashed out, pinned the tail.

The mouse squealed. High. Terrified. Its eyes stared up at her. For a moment, Cat observed it calmly, almost lazily. Her other paw cuffed the creature gently. Its head jerked sideways. She cuffed it again. The mouse squealed again.

She half raised her imprisoning paw. The mouse stayed frozen for a second, then gathered itself to run.

Cat sprang, and sank her sharp front teeth into the mouse's neck. It jerked once, then went still.

Cat contemplated the small body complacently.

"Well, what's this?" A cheerful voice broke into her absorption. "Caught a mouse, did you? Clever puss. We can use a good mouser in this house." Mistress Grove bent down to give her an approving pat, but Cat didn't feel it.

She had killed a mouse. She had toyed with it, then killed it. She had enjoyed killing it.

She had acted like a cat. But she wasn't a cat. She was a girl. She was Catrina Ashdale. She was. She was. She *was.*

She looked back at the mouse and shuddered.

Garth walked into the kitchen. "Have you seen cat?"

"Indeed I have, and the good puss has just caught a mouse."

"A mouse?" Garth echoed blankly. He followed the cook's eyes. "Oh, cat!" He stared at her, dark-ringed eyes dismayed. She stared back dismally.

"What's this?"

Garth jumped, then turned slowly to face his grandfather.

Cat had never seen Master Spellman in the kitchen before. Nor had she seen him less than impeccably groomed. Yet here he was, strolling into the room in his dressing gown, with his hair dishevelled from sleep. And it was almost noon.

"Here, I'll get you your breakfast, sir," Mistress Grove

said. "You go sit down in the dining room, and it will be ready in the blink of an eye."

"No, no – no need to disturb the day's routine. I ate well last night. I'll just help myself to a cup of kala, if I may. What's the commotion about?"

"Puss here has caught a mouse." The cook sounded as proud as though she had done the deed herself.

"So the cat has its uses. Maybe she'll catch more and earn her keep."

"No!" Horror rang in Garth's voice.

"No?" Master Spellman raised his eyebrows. "You don't want the cat to catch mice?"

"No! She mustn't. She can't."

The wizard stared at his grandson, an arrested look on his face, then switched his attention to Cat. She gazed at the floor, but felt his eyes watching her, studying her. If only she could disappear down the mouse hole. Finally he looked away.

"I would have thought you would be pleased that the cat you seem so fond of has done something to earn herself a welcome, Garth. But undoubtedly you have your reasons."

Master Spellman helped himself to a cup of kala and stood sipping it. Garth looked at the floor. Mistress Grove tossed the dead mouse onto the fire. Cat watched the flames consume the small body.

"You seem tired," Master Spellman said suddenly.

After a moment, Garth muttered, "I didn't sleep well."

"No? Something on your mind, perhaps?"

Garth said nothing.

"Your lack of sleep didn't hamper your work this morning, I trust."

"No."

"Hmm." Master Spellman finished his drink and set down his cup. "I'll go and get dressed. Please tell your mother I won't be home for lunch. I have a meeting."

Garth's head jerked up at the word meeting. "Wait."

Master Spellman turned back. "Yes?"

"I have a message for you. From Master Wishbe."

Cat's breath caught. Was Garth...? Surely he wouldn't tell his grandfather he knew about the conspiracy.

"From Danlo Wishbe? Where did you see him?" Master Spellman's voice was sharp.

Garth's hesitation was fractional. "In front of The Pelican's Nest. I went there last night. To listen to the music." He met his grandfather's eyes steadily. "He was hurrying past, but stopped when he saw me. He said to tell you to meet him the night the winners of the music competition were announced, at the same place and time as you were to meet last night. And to bring fifty gold pieces with you."

"That was all?"

"Yes."

"I see," the wizard said slowly, but his eyes remained on his grandson's face. A frown puckered his brow. "Thank you for delivering the message," he said politely, and turned away.

Cat breathed again.

They were safe. For now. But what would happen when the two wizards met? When Master Wishbe told the other man that his grandson had been not at The Pelican's Nest but at The Merry Jug and knew all about the plot, that his grandson's cat had been there too – the same cat that had overheard their earlier conversation, the same cat that Master Spellman had just scrutinized so thoroughly?

Master Spellman might make sure that no harm befell his grandson. But what about a cat/girl who knew too much?

THE DAY DRAGGED BY. Cat stayed in the kitchen. Every time she started to doze, she jerked herself awake. She didn't dare sleep. What if she woke again with her cat instincts uppermost?

What if she remained a cat for another month? Two? Would she become more and more a cat? Would her real self fade? Die?

What if she remained in her cat body forever?

Master Spellman was still out. Cat crept into the study, needing to be with someone who knew she was a girl. A book was open in front of Garth, but he was staring into space. He greeted her with a weary smile.

"I've been sitting here trying to think. Do you have any ideas? About what we should do, I mean."

She did, but she didn't think he would like them. Nevertheless, she jumped onto the desk and pointed to some letters.

He shook his head. "No. I can't tell someone."

She pointed to more letters.

"Captain kill Gayland," he read. He was still for a long minute. "You're right. I didn't think... I guess I didn't want to. But it adds up, doesn't it? A hot-tempered Uglessian. A Uglessian knife. Captain Penner could hide a weapon on himself and use it in the commotion that's sure to follow your father's song. And blame it on a Uglessian. Then we'd arrest that man, of course, and the other Uglessians would be furious. We'd call them bloodthirsty and they'd call us treacherous. As for the Islandians, they'd be so disgusted with both of us that they'd vow never to have anything more to do with either Freyans or Uglessians."

He looked at her wildly. "This is worse, far worse, than I thought."

She meowed and stared at him.

"No. I can't. I can't, even so. Oh Freyn." Garth covered his face with his hands.

She knew how he felt. She had been through the same dilemma. But Gayland's life was at stake. She meowed again and pawed his sleeve.

Garth removed his hands. "Yes, I know. Your father. I haven't forgotten. I'll have to warn him. We'll go now. Grandfather will have a fit when he finds out I've left my work unfinished, but why should I care what he thinks?" He rose. Cat jumped to the floor.

On his way to the door, Garth stopped suddenly. "Cat! I just realized...your father won't sing his song after we've warned him. And there's not time for them to find another musician. Everything will be all right." His voice shook with excitement.

It was as though a heavy stone that had been dragging her to the bottom of a pond had been removed. Cat purred. Garth laughed and lifted her in his arms, giving her an affectionate hug. They left the room.

Only to meet Konrad Spellman in the hall.

"Were you going somewhere?" The wizard was removing his damp cloak.

"I'm going out," Garth said.

"Ah. You've undoubtedly completed your work, then."

"No."

"No? But you were planning to leave? On an important errand, no doubt."

"I *am* planning to leave. On a very important errand."

Master Spellman's eyes narrowed. "And what errand might that be?"

Garth hesitated. *Careful, Garth, careful,* Cat warned silently.

"I'm going to see someone."

"And who might this 'someone' be?"

"A musician."

Cat shut her eyes.

There was a long silence. "A musician?" Master Spellman asked at last.

"Yes." Garth took a deep breath. Cat felt it shudder through him. "I'm going to be a musician, not a wizard." Cat could hear and feel Garth's heart thumping like a maddened hare.

"This is a rather sudden decision, is it not?" Master Spellman's voice was surprisingly mild. Cat opened her eyes.

"No. I've always wanted to be a musician. It's only because of you –" Garth stopped.

"Only because of me that you're studying magic? I see." Master Spellman's voice was still mild. "Well, we'll discuss the matter later. I don't want to delay you from accomplishing your – very important errand." He stepped aside to let his grandson pass.

Garth remained rooted to the floor. Finally, he walked slowly towards the door. As he reached it, his grandfather said, "By the way, Garth –"

Garth stopped. "Yes?"

"I ran into Danlo Wishbe myself today."

Cat's heart lurched. Garth stood, motionless.

"I told him you had relayed his message faithfully, and he sent his thanks."

"That was kind of him," Garth said after a moment.

"The strange thing is, I met him at the same place you did last night."

Garth whirled. "What? Why – I mean, where...?"

"Why, in front of The Pelican's Nest, of course."

Garth stared at him.

His grandfather raised his eyebrows. "That *is* where you said you saw him, isn't it?"

Garth swallowed. "Yes. Yes, of course."

"I won't keep you any longer. Freyn's Day to you." His eyes fell on Cat. "To you both."

He strolled towards the study. Garth stared after him, then turned and fumbled for the door handle.

The rain had stopped, but the air was still moist. It

smelled of damp earth, green grass, and sausage and fish and onions and other food, newly cooked as food-stall owners emerged into the rain-washed streets. But Cat was aware of these smells only at the edge of her mind. A question consumed her.

Had Master Spellman's words been spoken innocently? Or was he playing a game with them, the same cat-and-mouse game she had played earlier that day?

# Minstrel's Choice

GAYLAND WAS COMING OUT THE DOOR AS they walked up Threadmore Street. He hailed them cheerfully.

"Freyn's Day, my musical friends. Come for more songs? I was going out, but –"

"No. We've come to talk to you."

Gayland's lips quivered. "We? You and the cat? Well, why not? As I started to say, I can postpone my errand. Come upstairs."

"No. We...I mean, *I* need to talk to you alone. Can we go somewhere quiet?"

Gayland's eyebrows shot up. "Alone? But –"

"Please. It's important."

Gayland hesitated. Garth added, in a low voice, "It's about the competition. About the wizards' council."

All trace of amusement left the musician's face. He studied Garth, then said curtly, "Very well. There's a deserted house with a garden not far from here. We'll go there."

A crumbling brick wall surrounded the garden. Cat jumped it with ease, then watched her father and Garth scramble over it. The garden was small and tangled, overgrown with vines and brambles. Cat picked her way through them with care and stopped beside a low stone bench. A pool of rainwater lay in the middle. Garth and Gayland sat down gingerly on either end.

"Now, what's this about the council?" Gayland demanded. He didn't sound particularly friendly.

Garth paused, a swimmer at the edge of deep water, then plunged in. "You mustn't do it."

"What?"

"You must not sing your song, the one that insults the Uglessians, I mean. It's not just that it will harm Freya – though it will, you must know it will. But it's not safe for you. You're doing it because of Lucia, aren't you? You need money so she can get the food and rest she needs. But –"

"Just what do you know about all this? Or think you know? And how?" Gayland was eyeing Garth as though the boy were a friendly dog that had suddenly turned rabid.

"We...I overheard your conversation with Master Wishbe at The Merry Jug. Then after you left, two other men joined him."

Gayland's eyebrows rose. "Overheard? You just happened to overhear our conversation?"

"Yes. Well, no. I... But that can wait. What can't wait is... They plan to kill you."

Gayland listened in silence as Garth outlined the conclusions he and Cat had reached. At the end, Garth said earnestly, "So you see why you can't be there that night."

Gayland shook his head. "I still don't understand how you came to know all this, but I suppose it doesn't matter. It was kind of you to warn me. But do you think me so naive that I didn't foresee this danger?"

Garth stared at him. So did Cat. "You mean...you knew they'd plan to kill you?"

Gayland shrugged. "It seems logical. That's one of the reasons I demanded most of my pay before I sang."

"But... You can't mean...you don't want to die, surely."

"Oh no. I love life too well to want to leave it. But forewarned is forearmed, they say. I'll be on guard for a knife in my back. And your information helps, lad. You say this Captain Penner will have the knife. What does he look like?"

"He's tall, with wide shoulders and a yellow moustache that swirls upwards at both ends. He has blue eyes and full lips. I think he's quite young, in his late twenties, maybe. I'm sorry. I couldn't get a clear view of his face. He wore a hood, and it was dim."

Gayland nodded. "Thank you. That will help."

"But you can't –"

"I must. As you said, I need the money for Lucia."

"But –"

"No." Gayland's voice shook with fierce, determined passion. "I will not let her die. Not if there is anything I can do to stop it. Nor will I delay finding a place where she can rest quietly while she heals. A friend tells me there's a vacant cottage in Applegarth, with a sunny garden filled with apple and pear trees. It's what we've dreamed of. With the money I'll get next week, plus what I've already received, we can afford it."

Garth swallowed. "It won't do you much good if you're dead."

"It will do Lucia good. Oh, I've every intention of staying alive. But if I die, at least she'll be safe and well. No," he said as Garth opened his mouth, "don't argue. I've chosen my path, and I won't change it now."

He was quiet for a while, then said slowly, "All my life, I've deserted people I love, who love me. I left my home when I was young. I had two brothers who could help my parents on their farm. I told myself I wouldn't be missed. All I wanted to do was wander the roads and sing my songs. I told my family I would keep in touch, but...well, I was busy, and happy. When I finally returned, my parents were dead and my brothers and I had little in common. I've never been back."

He fell silent again. The tall grass prickled against Cat's fur. She moved slightly, then was still. Gayland said softly, "There was a woman I loved. Lianna, her name was. She was lovely, and loving. Our lives were filled with joy and laughter, especially after our daughter was born."

He sighed, then went on. "It ended, as everything else ended. Lianna said our child needed security – a home, family, roots. She gave me an ultimatum, finally. Them or the wandering life, she said. And I chose the wandering life, forsaking my love, forsaking my responsibility. I've often wondered how they're doing. There were times, especially in the early days, when I thought about going to see them, but

I could never face the pain of knowing it would only be a fleeting visit. My little girl – Catrina, we called her – must be fifteen now." He was quiet, staring at a rose bush grown wild and thorny beside the bench.

Cat's throat hurt. Part of her longed to cry, "Father! It's me!" Another part wanted to shrink shyly behind the bench. She felt Garth's eyes on her, but refused to meet them.

Gayland shook himself, as though shaking off a dream. "But that's the past. Lucia is the present. My present. I will not lose her. And I will not give up my responsibility. Not again." He smiled wryly. "Rather late to be assuming responsibility, isn't it? If I don't watch out, I'll be donning sober respectability next. I might even join the Musicians' Guild and live like a smug, prosperous merchant."

Garth was still looking down at Cat. "What about your responsibility to Freya?" he asked in a low voice.

Gayland grimaced. "I've never concerned myself much with matters of state. It's not that I don't care for my country. Freyn knows I've sung all the old heroic songs, time and again. What minstrel hasn't? But who's to say for sure that Master Wishbe's not right when he thinks we should keep our distance from our neighbours? Anyway, Freya's not my responsibility. Lucia is."

Not his responsibility? Cat stirred uneasily.

"So you see why I must continue on my course, no matter what the risk. What about you, lad? What will you do?"

Garth looked at him. "Me?"

"Will you tell someone? The magistrates? The army?"

Garth shook his head mutely.

"No? What about *your* responsibility to Freya?" Gayland's voice held more than a touch of mockery.

Hot colour swamped Garth's face. He turned away. "I suppose I'm like you. A person means more to me than my country."

Gayland waited, but the boy said nothing more.

"I see. Well, I presume that's all we have to discuss then. Again, my thanks for your warning." Gayland rose and walked away. He had one leg over the crumbling wall when Garth called, "Wait."

The musician paused.

"I won't tell anyone, but I will try to stop you. I *will* stop you. Somehow."

Gayland laughed. "Fair warning, is it? Very well." He waved a cheery hand and swung his other leg over the wall. A moment later, Cat heard his light footsteps walking away. Then the only sounds were the drone of a nearby bee and the distant hum of carts and voices. She stared sightlessly in front of her.

Garth's hand, slamming down on the bench, made her jump. "I said I'd stop him, and I will. If only I could think... Can you think of a way?"

Reluctantly, she shook her head.

Garth sighed. "We still have ten – no, nine – days till the council. And if we haven't come up with an answer before then...well, we'll have to stop them on the night itself. Somehow."

Somehow.

Perhaps she could leap at Captain Penner. Claw him. Make him drop his knife. She would enjoy clawing him.

"I'll ask Grandfather if we'll be allowed into the council hall," Garth said. He looked at Cat. "At least I know your name now. Catrina. Cat," he said tentatively, and laughed. "I wasn't so far wrong, was I?"

The dinner hour was long past. Cat's mouth watered at the smell of food as they walked through the golden evening light. Nevertheless, she was as reluctant to return to 6 Gotham Street as Garth seemed to be, and didn't protest when he took a detour along the busy waterfront.

"It will be even busier in a week or so as everyone gathers for Midsummer," Garth predicted, dodging out of the way of a passing cart.

From her perch on Garth's shoulder, Cat watched a trio of sailors swagger by, jingling the coins in their pockets. Then, just as Garth was rounding a corner that led away from the harbour, she spied a tall figure, half turned away. A profile.

It was...

No. It couldn't be. What would Kenton Herd be doing in Freyfall? He'd be home, minding his crops and herds. Resolutely, she refused to think of him all the way home.

Annette Spellman was descending the stairs as they entered the house. "You're late," she greeted her son.

He nodded absently. "Is Grandfather here?"

"He's in the study."

Garth swallowed. "Is he very angry?"

"With you? He doesn't seem to be. In fact –" Annette

179

shook her head, bewildered, "he told *me* not to be angry when you failed to show up for dinner. He said you'd told him you had an important errand to do."

Garth blinked. "Oh." He headed for the study.

"I told Ellen to keep your dinner warm. It's waiting for you in the kitchen."

"Thank you," Garth said over his shoulder. He halted in front of the closed study door, then knocked firmly.

"Come in," Master Spellman called. "Ah, Garth, so you're home. Did you have a pleasant visit with your musician friend?"

"Yes. That is...not really."

"No?" His grandfather raised his eyebrows.

"No, but that's not... I want to ask you something."

His grandfather waited.

"The council – the council of wizards – who will be allowed to attend?"

"Whoever has received an invitation."

"Oh," Garth said. Cat's heart plummeted.

"Why?"

"Why? Well, I was hoping I could be there. Can I? As your apprentice? Just to watch?"

"But why this interest in a wizards' gathering? I thought I heard you announce your intention of becoming a musician earlier today." Master Spellman watched his grandson through narrowed eyes. Again, Cat remembered her game with the mouse.

"I want...that is, it's because of the music. The best musicians in Freya will sing on the opening night."

Cat hoped it wasn't as obvious to Master Spellman as it was to her that Garth had scrambled for his answer.

"Ah, I see. I'm afraid I must dash your musical hopes. As I said, only those who've been invited – master wizards, Queen Elira and her advisers, and our guests from Uglessia and Islandia – will be allowed in. And the winning musicians, of course. The guards have strict instructions to deny entry to all others."

Cat swallowed.

"Is there anything else? No? Then, if you'll excuse me, I have work to do." Master Spellman's head bent over the papers on his desk.

Garth left the room, Cat still riding his shoulders, and closed the door carefully behind him. "I'd rather he explode than be so polite," he muttered as he trudged up the stairs.

Inside his room, Garth sank onto his bed. "Now what?"

Cat didn't know. She jumped up to the window ledge and sat looking at the garden, darkened by lengthening shadows. If she'd thought it might work, she would have beaten her head against the window to batter an idea into it.

Garth sighed. "I suppose we should eat."

Despite her earlier hunger, Cat's stomach felt too tight to enjoy the scraps Mistress Grove put out for her. Konrad Spellman's words kept pounding in her head, like echoes bouncing off the walls of a dark cave: "...only those who've been invited – master wizards, Queen Elira and her advisers, and our guests from Uglessia and Islandia – will be allowed in. And the winning musicians, of –"

The winning musicians!

She raced up the stairs, then waited impatiently for Garth to appear and open his bedroom door. She leapt onto the night table where the written alphabet lay waiting.

Garth's face brightened when he saw where she sat. "You have an idea?" Leaning over, he deciphered the letters she pointed to.

"You...compete," he read slowly. "What do you mean?"

She pointed to other letters.

"Music...competition." He drew back. "Me? Compete in the music competition? Are you mad?"

She stared at him, challenged him.

"Yes, I know. I said I'd stop them. And I know it's a way of getting inside. But you don't understand. The best musicians in Freya have been planning for this for months. Even if I were an experienced musician, how could I compete? How could I have any hope of winning?"

She continued to stare.

"Cat, you're mad. The competition trials are four days away."

She gazed at him, unblinking. Finally, he sank onto his bed and groaned. "All right, Cat. You win. I must be as mad as you are. I'll try."

# THE SONG

FROM HER POSITION, CURLED UP AT THE FOOT of Garth's bed, Cat watched Garth stare vacantly at the sheets of paper in front of him. The candle guttering beside him threw hollow shadows onto his face.

It was late. The house had long since fallen asleep. For the last three hours, the only sound Cat had heard had been the scratch of Garth's pen.

"Oh Freyn!" Garth scrunched the papers into a ball and flung them at the wall. A moment later, candle extinguished, he crawled into bed.

Cat lay still, very aware of Garth as he shifted restlessly from side to side. Was he right? Was she mad? Was she asking the impossible?

What was the alternative?

Could she climb onto the palace balcony, slip through an open window, spring at Captain Penner as he drew his knife? But where could she hide? If seen, she would be thrown out.

She forced her eyes to close, but sleep came slowly. Next morning, a scum of tiredness dulled her mind and senses. She came to alert attention, though, as she passed the dining room where the Spellmans sat at breakfast.

Garth cleared his throat. "I won't be studying magic for the next few days," he announced loudly.

Cat stopped. Cautiously, she poked her head inside the room. Garth sat, head high, shoulders back. His expression reminded Cat of Ambrose Whitefalls, who collected honey from the wild bees that made their homes in the groves around Frey-under-Hill. Master Whitefalls wore that same look of wary determination as he approached a hive. And something else, something Cat had never seen on Garth's face before, the look of one who knew just what he was doing.

Annette had been lifting a cup to her lips. At Garth's words, hot kala splashed onto her hand. Hastily, she set the cup down and darted an anxious glance at her father-in-law.

He, however, only raised his eyebrows. "Indeed? And what will you be doing instead, if I may ask?"

"Writing a song."

Alarm sprang into Annette's face. "Garth —"

"I see. And is there a reason why this song must be written in the next few days?" Master Spellman asked politely.

Garth's hands were clenched so tightly around the cup they held that Cat wondered why it didn't shatter. "I'm going to enter the music competition."

Silence. Then Annette brushed a hand in front of her, as though clearing away smoke. "Garth, this is ridiculous. You're an apprentice wizard, not a minstrel. Oh, I know you love music, but... Do you realize there are only three days till the competition begins? Do you know how many musicians will compete? How many good musicians?"

Garth swallowed. "Yes."

"Then...are you feeling all right? The summer fever..." She reached out to feel his forehead. Garth jerked back.

"I'm fine, Mother!"

She flinched.

"I'm sorry," Garth said more gently. "But I'm not sick. It's just that this is important."

"There seem to be many important matters in your life these days," Master Spellman observed. He placed his napkin on the table and rose. "Don't fret, Annette. I'm sure Garth has a good reason for his actions – or thinks he does."

He started towards the door. Too late, Cat drew back.

Konrad Spellman looked back at his grandson. "Perhaps your friend here can help with the song. Provide some inspiration, perhaps. It certainly seems to have – inspired – you in other ways."

Garth flushed. Cat's stomach tightened into a cold knot. More and more, she was sure the wizard knew something. But what?

Hours later, she only wished she *could* help Garth with his song. But she couldn't. True, tunes had wandered in and out of her mind all her life. But she'd never learned to read or write music, and she doubted that the sounds a cat could make would be helpful. Anyway, she was as bereft of words and ideas as Garth seemed to be.

Garth surveyed the litter of paper before him. "Not a single phrase or note that's worth anything. Nothing! I used to dream of writing music. When I was supposed to be studying or listening to Grandfather, songs would come unbidden. I was always getting into trouble because of it. And now, when I do have the time, when so much depends on it... Nothing."

He rose abruptly. "I need to get out of here. Coming?"

Silently, she padded after him.

As the warm sun stroked her fur and the streets hummed around her, Cat's nerves began to relax. Their desultory ramblings brought them to the harbour again. Cat scanned each passing face, just in case she really *had* seen Kenton Herd yesterday. None were his. None even resembled his. Of course not.

"Look," Garth said, and pointed.

A ship was nosing into place beside the others lined up along the pier. It bore the royal standard, Cat saw. But not *just* the royal standard. Below the blue and silver emblem was a circular flag, with nine green islands arranged against a background of blue.

"Islandia," Garth breathed. "It must be the Islandian delegation."

Others had reached the same conclusion. A crowd gathered and stood watching as the boat docked and its passengers descended. Four women and two men. One of the men...

Cat gasped. Master Weaver! Instinctively, she drew back. But that was silly. Even if he noticed her, the old wizard wouldn't recognize her.

Behind her, a child said loudly, *"They're* not special. I thought they'd be special."

The girl was hushed instantly, but Cat agreed with her. There was nothing distinctive, nothing exotic, about the people who stood watching their luggage come ashore. Except for Master Weaver and one woman, they had darker hair and skins than most Freyans, but that was the only thing that set them apart. Cat had expected more from the legendary wise women of Islandia.

"There's Kerstin Brooks, who used to be Kerstin Speller."

Again, Cat was disappointed as she followed Garth's pointing finger to the woman with the fairer skin who stood among the Islandians. She was of medium height and build, and her hair, more grey than brown, was pulled into an untidy bun. She bore no resemblance to the heroic wizard of Cat's imagination.

The six passengers started to walk towards a waiting carriage. As they approached, Kerstin Brooks's eyes fell on Garth. She stopped.

"It's Garth Spellman, isn't it?"

Garth gave a jerky bow. "Yes, Mistress Brooks."

"How is your grandfather? Well, I hope."

"Yes, Mistress."

"And you? Working hard at your studies, I trust. I know your grandfather has great hopes for you."

Garth turned tomato red and mumbled an incoherent answer.

"Give my regards to your grandfather." The woman smiled

and moved on, accompanied by a tall, angular woman with a leathery old face and sharp black eyes, and a lean man with a shock of white in his raven-black hair.

Master Weaver walked beside two younger women. Or perhaps not women, for one, a slight girl with masses of dark curls who was gazing about her in awe, looked younger than Cat. She walked by, but her companion, a plump, pink-cheeked woman, jerked to a halt when she saw Cat. She stared for a moment, then went on, but her eyes stayed on Cat as the group got into the carriage and drove off.

*She knows. She knows I'm not a cat. What if she tells someone? What if she tells the wrong person?* Cold fingers moved down Cat's spine.

The crowd dispersed. Garth strode off, still red. They wandered through the streets, crowded with shoppers and stalls. Cat saw one she knew, the stall where Garth had purchased her flute. Garth had the flute with him now, in a pouch by his side.

*He'll find it hard to give it up. Well, maybe he won't have to. At this rate, I'll be a cat forever.*

As though echoing her thoughts, the sweet, high notes of a flute came from the street beyond. Garth brightened – he'd been glum since his encounter with Kerstin Brooks – and hurried towards it.

The flute player was a tall young man with long, moon-coloured hair. Cat's eyes widened. A Uglessian! She gazed in fascination as the six-fingered hands moved and tune after tune rippled out. By the time he ended, the grey cloak at his feet was flecked with bright copper.

Garth dug in his pockets, but only produced three coppers. "It would be an insult," he muttered, and thrust them back.

Beside him, someone snorted. "Insult, is it? Foolish, foolish."

Cat started. She knew that voice. She craned her neck and peered down at a tiny woman with sparse white hair, a wrinkled, toothless face, and a rainbow of mismatched rags.

It was Mab. Mab, who had been kind at a time when she needed kindness badly.

"He deserves more than three coppers. Much more," Garth protested.

"So if it be you has more next time you hear him, give more then. Every copper be precious if you be hungry."

Hastily, Garth dug in his pockets again and threw the coppers onto the cloak. He turned to go.

Cat gave a loud, plaintive meow and jumped from his shoulder, landing at Mab's feet. She rubbed against the old woman's legs, purring.

"Pretty puss," Mab crooned.

Garth stared. "She doesn't usually do that. It's almost as though she knows you."

"And so she may, so she may. Mab shares her crumbs with cats, when she has them to share, though I can't say as how I recollects this one."

"Mab," Garth said slowly. "I think that's the name Cat – that is, a girl I met – mentioned. She said a woman named Mab had shared her food with her."

"She did, did she? That was good of her. As I says, Mab shares her food, when she has it to share."

"But doesn't that leave you hungry?" Garth asked, eyeing the frail, stooped figure beneath its assortment of rags.

Mab shrugged, her bony shoulders moving up and down like twigs in the wind. "Us all needs a helping hand, now and then, and who's to know that better than Mab?" She bent, her aged knees creaking, and patted Cat. "Good puss." She straightened painfully. "I'd best be on me way."

Cat meowed. She stared hard at Garth.

He stared back, dismayed. "But, Cat, I can't. I don't have anything."

True. He'd just given away his last coins. But there was something... Cat hesitated. Then, resolutely, she climbed up Garth's right leg.

"Ow! Cat, what are you doing?"

She reached out a paw and tapped his pouch.

He looked at her blankly. "What?"

Annoyed, she hissed and tapped the pouch again. She could feel the hard, round shape of the flute beneath the cloth.

"The flute? Is that what –? But...are you sure?"

Cat leapt to the ground and nodded.

Garth rubbed his thigh, where her claws had dug in. "Really sure? You want me to sell the flute?"

Suppressing a spasm of regret, she nodded again.

Garth sighed. "All right. If you say so." He turned to Mab, who had been an interested spectator. "Come with us."

She cackled. "Oh, dearie, I don't knows what you be up to, but I wouldn't miss it for the world and all. I'se never seen a boy and cat talk to each other like that before."

Garth shortened his steps to match Mab's. Cat trotted beside them.

The stallkeeper examined the flute with interest. "Hmm. Looks familiar."

"It should. I bought it from you a fortnight ago. For one gold piece and three silver."

"Did you now? I'll give you seven silver coins."

"That's outright theft," Garth said angrily.

"A used flute isn't worth as much as a new one," the man pointed out.

"But I've never – well, hardly ever – even played it."

"That's what they all say."

"I'll sell it for one gold and two silver coins," Garth said, and the bargaining was on. In the end, they settled for nine silver coins. Cat felt as though she had cheated Garth out of four coins, but he looked satisfied enough as he held out the nine coins to Mab.

"Here, what's this, boy?"

"For you."

"I'se never had that many coins in me life. Why'd you go and sell your flute just to give me them? It be more than I needs."

"But not more than you deserve. Please take it, for the sake of the kindness you did my friend – and all the others you've helped."

Mab still hesitated.

"We all need a helping hand, now and then," Garth quoted softly.

"So we do. So we do. Well, I'll take the money then, and

Freyn's blessings on you, boy, yes, and on you too, cat, for it's plain as the nose on me face that it be you who wanted me to have the money, though I don't understand it." She took the coins. They disappeared like magic beneath the outer layer of rags. "But then, there be many things Mab doesn't understand. I do know good hearts when I meets them, though, and I thank you for them."

"And we thank you, Mab." Impulsively, Garth bent down and kissed the wrinkled cheek. Cat purred.

Mab raised a hand to her cheek. "Well, well, that be a prize worth all the coins in the world. A kiss from a handsome young man. Who'da thought it?" She cackled and walked away, cupping her cheek as though it were a fragile, exotic flower. Garth swung Cat onto his shoulders, a broad grin on his face. He started off, whistling.

He stopped abruptly. "That's it!"

Cat gave what she hoped was an enquiring meow.

"My song. That's what my song will be about."

Cat was puzzled.

"Mab. My song will be about Mab."

# THE COMPETITION

FOR TWO DAYS, GARTH STAYED IN HIS ROOM, emerging only for meals, and that reluctantly. Cat grew bored. Bored and irritated. She wanted to know how the song was progressing. She *needed* to know how it was progressing. But Garth refused to share it with her until it was finished. There was nothing for her to do but stare at his bent head and listen to the scratching of his pen. Eventually, she slipped away to enjoy the garden and explore the city.

If Freyfall had moved to a hectic beat before, Cat thought, it now ran with trills of laughter and leaping arpeggios of excitement. She watched stall owners attach streamers from the tops of their booths, shop owners scramble to their roofs, bright banners in hand. Every home and kala shop she passed held the mouth-watering smells of sweetmeats and spice cakes. Midsummer was coming, and people were flocking to the city to celebrate the festival and witness the historic meeting of wizards.

Then a new buzz of excitement throbbed through the city. Queen Elira's coach had been spotted. Cat joined a throng of people hurrying towards the palace. They were just in time to watch the royal blue and silver coach draw up and the queen step out.

Cat knew that Queen Elira was sixty. But her head, held high beneath a diadem of pearls and sapphires, was still crowned by rich auburn braids, and only faint lines of age marked her face as she smiled at her people. She wore a gown that sang of grace in the clean simplicity of its lines and the subtle blend of various shades of blue.

Other carriages drove up. Others emerged. They too were richly dressed. But Cat had eyes only for the queen.

"Strange she's never wed, despite her many suitors," muttered a woman behind Cat. Cat agreed. She watched Queen Elira mount the palace stairs. A captain of the guards sprang forward to open the door.

Captain Penner. Cat took an instinctive backwards step.

Queen Elira nodded graciously and entered the palace. A tall, heavy-set man dressed in plum satin came next.

"That's her cousin, Count Varic," announced a man in the crowd to anyone who cared to listen.

He didn't resemble her much, Cat thought, except for the auburn colour of his thinning hair. He drew out a handkerchief and mopped his face. Cat's eyes widened. He must be wearing at least ten ornate and flashy rings on the one hand. He exchanged a brief word with the captain, then he too entered.

The rest of the entourage followed and the door closed.

The flurry of activity stopped. The buzz of excitement died down. Slowly, reluctantly, the crowd left.

Cat slipped into the shadow of an overhanging eave and kept watch on the tall, green-uniformed man across the street. After two hours, she gave up. Captain Penner stood rigidly at attention, like the other guards. Occasionally, someone approached and was either admitted or turned away. Cat knew none of them. It was all very polite, and very boring.

She walked home, ignoring the gaiety swirling around her. But it was impossible to ignore the smells of Mistress Grove's Midsummer baking that met her as she jumped into the house through an open window. Cat sniffed hungrily as she padded upstairs.

Garth's door was closed. Cat scratched it to get his attention.

"What are you doing, you naughty cat? Scratching this good wood!"

Just her luck. Mistress Fairway had come up the stairs behind her. The housekeeper's face was red with anger.

The door opened. Garth stood there, pen in hand. The housekeeper turned on him.

"Look what your cat has done! Made scratch marks in this door."

"I'm sure they can be repaired," Garth said soothingly.

"Repaired! And what about the other trouble it's caused?"

"What trouble?" Garth asked blankly. Cat bristled.

"What trouble, he asks? This whole house has turned upside down since it arrived. And you! You've changed most of all. Worrying your poor grandfather into an early grave, that's what you're doing."

"He doesn't look that worried to me," Garth said.

"No? You've no eyes to see then, that's plain. I haven't seen him like this since your father got sick and died." Mistress Fairway stalked away. Garth gazed after her, a frown creasing his forehead. But the frown didn't last long. He motioned Cat inside.

"It's done," he announced. "Well, not completely done. I still have to make changes, make it better. But the main work's done. Do you want to hear it?"

What a question. She meowed and fixed him with her eyes. He picked up his lute and looked at her, a bit shyly. "It's called 'The Helping Hand,'" he said, and began.

He had said he would write a song about Mab, and so he had. He sang of Mab, old, wrinkled Mab, whose clothes were rags, whose food was stale bread, whose home was the streets. But there was no pathos in the song. The music captured the sounds of Freyfall: the vendors' cries, the rumble and creak of carts, the clatter of carriages, the babble of voices, the rush of the falls. Weaving in and out of this background was the melody, and that was clear and strong and loving, as Mab was clear and strong and loving, and ever ready to lend a helping hand.

That was the refrain, the helping hand that everyone, rich and poor, young and old, weak and powerful, needed to give and receive.

The music shifted. Cat could almost see the grey mountains Garth sang of, the stark, arid land. Then the helping hand reached out, softly, gently, with the patter of raindrops. The hand stretched back across the mountains, added fresh strands to Freyan life, as strong and tangy as kala.

The music changed again. Cat saw the sea, mist, dark hills emerging as the mist cleared. The hand held out a gift more prized than rubies, the Islandian gift of healing. Then the hand turned, gave back. Rousing winds from Freya blew away the entangling cobwebs of tradition and freed imprisoned talents.

The Mab theme wove through it all, strong and clear and loving.

When the notes died away, Cat sat still. She had never dreamed that Garth could write a song like this, a song that moved her close to tears.

"Do you like it?" he asked anxiously.

She nodded, then nodded again, vehemently.

His face relaxed. "Good. Well...time for dinner, I guess."

But later, as she tried to sleep, doubts crept in. Was Garth's composition as good as she thought, or was it just her memories of Mab that touched her? Was it good enough to win them entry to the council hall?

It had to be.


TWO MORNINGS LATER, they woke early and crept downstairs. Garth's hand was on the doorknob when Annette's voice made them both jump.

"Have you had breakfast?"

"No. I'm not hungry. I'd just...I couldn't eat."

"And cat? I suppose you're taking her with you. Shouldn't she have something to eat?"

"She's not hungry either."

His mother shook her head but didn't argue. "Wait a moment. I'll bring something you can eat later."

Annette was back in a couple of minutes, carrying a package. Garth stuffed it into the pack that held his lute.

"Freyn be with you, Garth. I know you'll do well."

A wave of surprised pleasure crossed his face. "Thank you. I'll do my best."

"I know." She leaned forward and kissed his cheek.

He hesitated, then reached out and hugged her tightly, like a small child clutching his mother for assurance in a dark night. Annette returned the hug, then stepped back and smiled at her son, her eyes moist.

THE MUSICIANS' GUILD HALL, the site for the competition, stood on the central island. Cat was glad of the walk. The morning sparkled, like sun on fresh dew, and the walk soothed her nerves.

The courtyard was half full when they arrived. A man with a dark pointed beard and jaunty red shirt grinned at Garth as the boy joined the outskirts of one circle. "You're here early, just like the rest of us. I suspect we've all made a mistake. It will be a long day."

"But who could sleep any longer, on a day that promises such fine music?" said the man next to him, and plucked at the strings of his harp till they screeched like a magpie.

Everyone laughed.

They waited. More and more musicians arrived. There must be – what? Two hundred? Three? Cat couldn't tell. She saw Mel. She did not see her father.

Finally, a man emerged from the hall. He held up a hand for silence, but there was no need. Everyone was still.

"You will break into six groups," he said. "A judge will hear all the musicians from one section, and choose the best five from it. The finalists will then appear before all six judges tomorrow. Will everyone whose name begins with A, B or C enter the hall, then go to the last room on the left. Those whose names begin..." He droned on.

Cat watched the first group enter the hall. Gayland was among them. She supposed she'd been foolish, hoping he'd have changed his mind.

Garth was stopped at the door. "You can't bring that cat in here."

"But I need... That is, she won't do any harm."

"No cats."

"Don't be so rigid," said a buxom woman behind Garth. "We all need our lucky charms at a time like this."

The man hesitated, then shrugged. "Very well."

At least forty people jammed inside the waiting room. Only a fortunate few had chairs. Garth sat on the floor, his back against a wall. Cat crouched beside him.

A thin man dressed in court livery stood beside the door. He cleared his throat imperiously. Everyone looked at him. "You will each have ten minutes to perform," he announced. "You will go first," he said to a gangling young man. The youth's Adam's apple bobbed nervously. "You," he said, nodding to the buxom woman, "come with me, so you'll be ready to go in as soon as he's finished."

Musician after musician was called. Some shrugged when they returned. Others grimaced. Still others boasted of how well they'd done.

A tall young woman with flame-red hair and a fine-boned face came back to find her chair taken. She glanced around, then seated herself on the floor beside Garth.

"Your cat is beautiful," she said after a moment.

"Thank you," Garth said shortly.

"Does your cat bring you luck? I have a luck stone that I carry with me always."

"Oh."

"Have you competed in a musical contest before?"

"No."

"It is hard on the nerves, is it not?"

Garth was silent.

The other waited a moment, then sighed. "If you do not like Uglessians, say so and I will move." She sounded tired, not angry.

Garth's head jerked to face her. So did Cat's.

"I'm sorry," Garth said. "I didn't mean...I didn't realize you're Uglessian till now. I certainly don't mind. It's just...I'm nervous, I suppose. I didn't mean to be rude."

The young woman smiled. "It is I who should apologize. I too do not like to talk when I am nervous. But then, when the worry is over, I talk too much."

"*Is* the worry over?"

She shrugged. "There is nothing more I can do now."

"But if it matters very much that you be chosen..." Garth's voice shook.

A small frown puckered her brow. "Yes." She looked away. "Yes."

Silence.

Garth broke it. "My name is Garth Spellman."

The girl – for she was just a girl, Cat realized, perhaps a year older than she was – smiled at him. "I am Talisa. Talisa Thatcher, I suppose you would call me here, though at home I am just Talisa, or sometimes Talisa of the red hair, or Talisa, daughter of Davvid, or granddaughter of Redelle." She hesitated, then added, "My grandmother and grandfather will be present at this wizards' council."

"So will my grandfather."

"We have much in common then."

The usher re-entered the room and cleared his throat. Garth's head spun towards him.

"Brandon Thornhill."

Garth's breath wheezed out.

Talisa laughed. "Your turn will come," she assured him.

Time passed. More names were called. Cat waited. And waited. Garth, she noticed sourly, didn't seem to mind the delay so much, now that he was busy chatting with Talisa.

"Garth Spellman."

Cat's heart thumped once, painfully, then settled to a dull pounding. She rose. So did Garth, slowly. He picked Cat up.

"Luck be with you," Talisa said.

"Thank you."

More waiting, this time on the other side of a heavy door. The usher looked dubiously at Cat but said nothing.

Finally, the door opened. A large florid man emerged, sweating profusely. He mopped his face and gave Garth a shaky smile. "Your turn."

Cat's stomach wobbled. She wondered how firm Garth's was.

The room, lit by the light from three tall, narrow windows, was bare except for a table and chair at the far end. Behind the table sat a small man with a receding hairline. He must have listened to over thirty singers already, but he looked neither tired nor bored, merely precise, judicial and – despite his small stature – intimidating. He nodded to a spot in the centre of the room. Cat retreated to a corner. The man ignored her.

"Your name?"

Garth cleared his throat. "Garth Spellman."

The man wrote this down. "The title of your song?"

"'The Helping Hand.'"

This was recorded as well. "Begin."

Garth did so. The lute sang clearly, precisely, but his voice quavered.

Cat shut her eyes. *Steady, Garth, steady.* It was hard, so hard, to sit here quietly, unable to help. Better, far better, to be singing.

After the first few notes, Garth's voice did steady. Cat's muscles relaxed slightly. She opened her eyes and studied the judge's face. It told her nothing.

When Garth ended, the man bent his head and wrote on

the sheet in front of him. Except for the scratching of his pen, the room was absolutely silent. For the first time, Cat was aware of how hot it was, with windows closed to bar any outside noise.

The judge looked up. "You may retire to the antechamber. The results will be announced after I've heard all the contestants."

"How did it go?" Talisa asked as Garth slid to the floor beside her.

"I don't know." After a moment, Garth added, his voice flat with despair. "I don't think he liked it."

The buxom woman overheard. "Don't sound so tragic, lad. The world won't end if you're not chosen."

"It might," Garth muttered. Talisa looked at him sharply, but said nothing. They sat in tense silence.

Late afternoon sun splashed the floor. A horse clattered by in the street outside. A cart rumbled past. Inside, there was a constant hum of voices. Despite the worry churning her stomach, Cat dozed.

Sudden quiet jolted her awake. Everyone in the room was sitting at alert attention, their eyes fixed on the man who had just entered, a sheet of paper in his hand. It was the judge.

"I have made my decision. The winners are: Sophie Wells –"

"Me!" squealed the buxom woman. The judge glanced at her. For the first time, a quiver of emotion showed on his face.

"Brandon Thornhill, Talisa Thatcher –"

Candles blazed in Talisa's eyes.

"Garth Spellman and..."

Cat paid no attention to the last name. It didn't matter. Nothing mattered except that Garth had been chosen. He had a chance. *They* had a chance. She heard no more. She doubted that Garth did either, not even the congratulations showered on him. He couldn't have looked more stunned had a falling beam struck him on the head.

In the courtyard, Cat spotted her father, but he was too far away for her to read his expression. Just as she was about to draw Garth's attention to him, a voice hailed them.

"Garth!"

It was Mel. He grinned at them. "I knew you'd enter the contest. And I see you still have that cat with you. I hope she brought you luck."

"Yes."

"Yes?" Mel's voice and eyebrows rose simultaneously. "You mean you were selected?"

Garth blinked twice. "Yes."

Mel slapped him on the back. "Good for you!"

Garth remembered his manners. "And you? Did you...?"

"No." Mel shrugged. "Oh well. Not my best effort, I admit. Serious themes are not my style. Come to The Lute so we can celebrate your victory in a suitable fashion."

"No, no, I... Thank you. No."

Mel laughed, slapped him on the back again, and departed. Gayland had disappeared.

Garth still seemed dazed as they walked home. Cat had to meow loudly several times to steer his wandering steps in the right direction. It was no wonder that Annette, after one look at her son's face as he entered the house, began to talk brightly about something completely unrelated to music.

"I'm a finalist," Garth said.

"What?"

"I'm a finalist," Garth repeated.

"Garth!" Annette's eyes shone. Pink blossomed in her cheeks. She flung her arms around him and hugged him.

"What's all this?" Konrad Spellman had emerged from his study.

Annette turned to him, beaming. "Garth was chosen to be one of the finalists."

Konrad's eyebrows shot up. "Really? I hadn't realized... Well, I suppose congratulations are in order, though I presume this does not guarantee you a performer's place at the council."

Excitement died in Garth's face. "No."

"It doesn't matter," Annette said. "What matters is that Garth was recognized as one of the best musicians in all Freya." But it did matter, of course. In the end, it was all that mattered.


THE NEXT DAY DAWNED cool and blustery. Annette, up at an early hour to wish her son Freyn's blessing, insisted that he take a cloak as well as the lunch she'd prepared.

Cat's eyes darted from person to person as they entered the Musicians' Guild courtyard. Gayland was not there. Her breath caught in sudden hope.

Then she saw him, sauntering through the open gate.

Her hope collapsed like a burst bubble.

Gayland surveyed the gathering. His eyes widened when he spotted Garth and Cat. He walked over to them and bowed gravely.

"An unexpected pleasure to see you both."

"Why unexpected?" Garth challenged. "Anyone can enter the contest."

"Indeed. You had given no indication of such an intention, however. Did you change your mind because you plan to deny me a chance to perform by winning one yourself?"

Garth met the other's eyes. "Why not?"

Gayland laughed. "May the best musician win, then. Freyn's luck to you. And to you, musical cat. Are you going to sing, too?" He laughed again, patted her, and strolled away. A moment later, the Guild Hall doors opened.

This time there were chairs enough for everyone. The antechamber was larger and there were fewer competitors. Garth smiled at Talisa when she sat beside him, but said nothing. Nor did she. Aside from a few low-voiced remarks here and there, the room was still.

The musicians were summoned alphabetically. Cat watched her father leave, then return. She waited. Name after name was called. Garth was almost last.

Six people – five men and one woman – sat behind a long oak table in the great hall, which was panelled in dark wood and lit by high windows. Cat studied them from her corner.

One of them, a bald man with spectacles perched halfway up his bulging nose, peered at her. "Why's that cat here?" he asked irritably.

Cat's muscles tensed.

Garth cleared his throat. "I never play without Cat present."

"Really?" asked the female judge. "Does the cat bring you inspiration?"

Garth flushed. "Not exactly. But –"

"Enough," interrupted the judge who Garth had played for the day before. "There's nothing in the rules that says a cat can't be present. Shall we begin?"

"Very well," said the man with the nose. "But keep it away from me. I can't abide the things."

Would he mark Garth more harshly because of her presence? Cat scarcely heard Garth's song. Worry gnawed her like a dog a bone. She was glad when Garth ended and she could escape.

Talisa Thatcher was next, followed by the two final contestants. Then they waited. Rain drummed against the windows.

Cat eyed her father, who sprawled in his chair, legs outstretched. He looked at ease. Confident. That didn't mean he'd be picked, Cat reminded herself. It *didn't*. So why should she feel so sick?

The door opened. Everyone's head snapped up, but only a liveried servant appeared.

"The judges require more time to reach their decision," he announced. Cat heard a muttered curse and several groans. "Retire to your dinners for now. The results will be posted on the Guild Hall door later tonight, as will instructions for the winners. The judges thank you for your efforts and commend you on your excellent songs."

"More waiting," grumbled a man with a trim black beard.

"And may we all have good appetites for our dinners," Gayland said wryly. He smiled at Garth and Cat and waved farewell.

Cat was carried home under Garth's cloak. She poked her head out from time to time, but there was little to see. Everything was grey. Grey and wet and dismal.

By early evening, the rain had stopped and pale sunlight filtered through the clouds that still threatened moisture. As they headed once again for the Guild Hall, Cat's mood was as black-edged as the clouds.

The paper was already posted on the main door. People stood in front of it, jostling each other as they tried to get a better view. Cat's eyes leapt from face to face.

Gayland was there. He stood looking at the list, then turned and walked away. Success? Failure? She couldn't tell.

Garth stopped. "I can't look. I just can't. I know I wasn't chosen. You look, Cat."

Did he think this didn't matter as much – no, more – to her as to him? Cat glared at him, but he didn't see. His eyes were closed. Back arched, tail straight up, she wove her way though the thicket of legs to the front.

Five names were printed in large black letters.

GAYLAND BELLMORE

She shut her eyes.

She had known. She had told herself he might not be, but she had known he would be a winner. What she had to find out was whether Garth had been chosen as well.

GAYLAND BELLMORE

DENYS GLOVER

WENDELL HARPER

GARTH SPELLMAN

TALISA THATCHER

Cat hadn't known she was holding her breath till she felt it rush out like liquid from a punctured wineskin. She hurried back to Garth.

He still hovered at the edge of the crowd, looking sick. She meowed as loudly and reassuringly as she could.

Garth didn't seem reassured. She meowed again, then swatted his leg.

"Cat, I can't. Let's go home."

She swatted again. This time she didn't sheathe her claws.

"Cat, stop! I... Oh, all right, I'll come."

Slowly, as though walking into a raging gale, Garth approached the notice. He stood in front of it and stared, his face white.

The man next to him glanced at him and said, "Never mind, lad. It's an honour to get this close."

Garth's head turned towards him. He blinked. "Yes. Yes, of course." His eyes returned to the notice. He stood there a long time, while those around him came and went.

Finally, he stirred. "It really is true. I can scarcely believe it, but..." Colour rushed back into his face. "Let's go home. I want to tell Mother."

They turned to go. As they did, Cat saw someone. She froze.

It couldn't be. It couldn't be, but it was. Making her way towards them, her hand on Kenton Herd's arm, was her mother.

# FAMILIES

LIANNA AND KENTON WALKED SLOWLY, THEIR eyes searching the faces around them. Lianna's gaze rested a moment on Cat, then moved on.

Cat was rigid. She stared at her mother. Swallowed. Swallowed again. Then, as though released from a holding spell, she streaked through and around the legs surrounding her until she was close enough to see and hear her mother clearly.

"She's not here." Lianna's voice was strained, like rope pulled to breaking point. Her hand clenched tightly on Kenton's arm.

"She must be. Master Weaver was sure of it."

"She may have come and gone. If only we'd got here sooner. If only we'd visited Master Weaver earlier. If only –"

"Hush now, my love. We're lucky. We're lucky the boatman could tell us where Cat had gone. We're lucky Master Weaver is in Freyfall for the council. And even if we missed her here, we know from Master Weaver's spell that she's safe and well."

"Do we? How come he couldn't see her, only sense her presence?"

"After weeks of looking, at least we know for certain she's in Freyfall. We'll find her, never fear."

Lianna said nothing. Her dark-rimmed eyes continued to search. Her clothes hung loosely on her. Cat's stomach hurt.

A man standing in front of the notice moved aside with a curse and a shrug. Lianna's eyes swept over it, then stopped.

"Kenton, look!"

"What is it?"

"Gayland. He's one of the chosen musicians."

Kenton whistled. "An honour indeed. He must be good."

"Yes, but don't you see what it means? Gayland must have been here. And that's why Cat was here. She must be with him."

"So she found him. That's more than we've managed to do, despite all our efforts. Now we know she's not wandering the streets." Kenton's face relaxed into a broad smile. Until then, Cat hadn't realized how tight it had been.

Lianna's eyes were bright. "Yes. And we know where Gayland will be two nights from now. We can wait for him outside the palace. Cat may even be with him." Her voice shook. Kenton's arm wrapped around her shoulders. Cat's eyes stung.

"Cat!" Garth's voice, close at hand, made Cat jump. It had an even more dramatic effect on Lianna and Kenton. Their heads jerked around. Their eyes hunted frantically for the person calling that name, for the person bearing that name. Then Lianna's gaze found Garth, stooping to lift Cat.

"Cat, why are you still here? I thought you were following me till I glanced around and you weren't there. Come on. It's time to go."

Cat struggled to free herself.

"Ow! Cat, what do you think you're doing?" Garth held Cat securely in his left arm while he sucked his bloodied right hand. Cat wriggled. Garth tightened his grip. "Stop it, Cat."

Kenton chuckled. Garth looked up, flushing.

Kenton smiled at him. "She has a mind of her own, like most cats."

"She's beautiful," Lianna said softly.

Cat grew still. She even allowed Garth to carry her away without a fuss. Nothing would be gained by staying here. She couldn't talk to her mother. She couldn't erase the worry from her face.

All the same, Garth had no right to pick her up and bear her off against her will. He had no right to treat her as though she really were a cat, not a girl. Resentment simmered in her and boiled over as Garth entered his home and let out a victory whoop.

Annette appeared at the top of the stairs.

"I'm in! I'm one of the five!"

Annette stared at her son, mouth agape. "Garth, you're not... You really mean it? You were chosen?"

He nodded.

"One of the best musicians in Freya? Garth, I always knew you loved music, but I never... Oh, Garth!" She ran down the stairs and hugged him.

The commotion brought others to the hall. Ellen, Della, and Mistress Grove beamed. Even Mistress Fairway bestowed a thin smile on Garth.

*Look at Garth. Enjoying his triumph. Basking in his mother's love. Doesn't he care that we still have to stop the plot? That my father's life is in danger? That I'm a cat?*

Master Spellman's voice cut through the jubilation like a knife through butter. "So. I must congratulate you, I see. Garth Spellman, master musician."

Annette's smile faltered. She hesitated, then turned and confronted her father-in-law. "Perhaps Garth should become a musician, since he's so talented."

"You believe he should abandon his study of wizardry, then?"

"I...he's always loved music."

Konrad Spellman waited. Annette took a deep breath. "Yes."

"I see. And what do you want to do, Garth?" His tone was neutral.

Garth was silent for a long minute. Finally he muttered, "At least I can make music. I can't make spells."

"That's not what I asked."

"All I want to do right now is sing on Midsummer Night."

"Ah, yes. That does seem important to you, doesn't it? I wonder why."

Garth said nothing, just stared at his grandfather. Konrad Spellman stared back. Cat could read nothing in his face.

"Of course it's important," Annette said. "It's a great honour to sing before the queen."

"Yes, of course. Foolish of me to think there might be another motive." Konrad's eyes dropped to Cat. "Do you plan to take this cat with you?" he asked politely.

Garth flushed. "Yes."

"I'll drop a word in Captain Penner's ear, then. Otherwise there might be objections to bringing a cat inside the palace."

He knew. She was sure he knew. Why did he want her there? She watched the wizard return to his study, her heart thumping like a fleeing hare.

She escaped to the garden. She needed to be alone. Away from Garth. Garth, who was happy.

She tried to think about Konrad Spellman. When he told Captain Penner to let her in, would he also tell him she was a girl, not a cat? Had he already told the captain and the other conspirators?

She stared in front of her but saw, not the blades of grass, not even Master Spellman's face, but her mother's weary eyes, lines of stress.

No. She must think. She must plan.

Lianna looked as though she hadn't slept well for days. For weeks.

*Think. Think. How can I stop them? What must I do when Captain Penner draws his knife?*

She shouldn't be here. She should be at home, at Ashdale, sitting on a flat stone by the brook, listening to its music.

Even if she were home, she wouldn't be at Ashdale. She would be on Kenton's farm, with Kenton.

So? What was wrong with that? Kenton was kind. He cared.

She should never have run away, only to be trapped in a cat's body, in a dangerous web of conspiracy.

If she hadn't run away, she would never have met Garth.

Why should that matter? Garth didn't care about her. All that interested him was his music.

But if she hadn't run away, she would never have met her father.

Gayland didn't care about her either. Lucia was the only one he loved.

Maybe. But after she saved his life, after he knew who she was, he would love her.

*If* she could save his life. *How* could she save his life?

And there she was, back on her treadmill of worry and fear.

She stayed outside until the long summer twilight deepened into true dark. She didn't want to see Garth. She very definitely didn't want to see, or be seen by, Konrad Spellman.

Unfortunately, he was the first person she met after she slipped through the door Ellen had left ajar to catch the breeze. The candle by the stairs outlined the wizard's tall form standing near the front door. Cat started to retreat, but there was no need. Konrad opened the door and left without seeing her.

Of course. This was the night Gayland was to meet with the conspirators.

She raced up the stairs and scratched at Garth's door. After a moment, Garth opened it, looking as befuddled as a sheep lost in the fog. Or a boy lost in his dreams, Cat thought bitterly.

"Where have you been?" Garth asked absently, then went back to sitting on his bed and staring into space.

Cat meowed. He paid no attention. Anger moved in her. She jumped onto the bedside table and patted the alphabet sheet, meowing loudly.

"What? Oh, you want to tell me something." Garth dragged himself out of his reverie and bent over the table.

"Merry...Jug. What? Oh, yes. They were to meet there tonight, weren't they? Grandfather must be on his way there now."

Cat meowed again and patted his hand. He really looked at her this time.

"You think we should go there? But what if they spot us again?"

She shuddered, remembering the looming shadows, hooded faces, imprisoning hands. But what choice did they have? She pointed to the words, "We go."

Garth shook his head. "No. It's too dangerous. The information we'd gain isn't worth the risk."

He was a coward, Garth Spellman. Or maybe it just didn't matter to him. Now that he'd proved what a fine musician he was, why should he care about Freya, about Gayland, about her?

Well, she would go without him. She stalked over to the door and scratched to be let out. Why, oh why, did she have to wear a body that couldn't do the simplest things for itself, like open a door?

"Wait, Cat. I have an idea."

She ignored him and scratched again.

"Cat..." He bent to pick her up. She hissed at him, ears back, spine arched, tail high.

Garth drew back. "Very well. You don't want to hear my plan, that's clear."

He opened the door. She left. Down the stairs, out the back door, through the back railing, into the street.

Clouds hid any glimmer of star or moonlight. Cat's eyes adjusted automatically to the darkness, but she didn't like it. The night felt lonely. It felt...dangerous.

What if she were discovered? Master Wishbe might dismiss her as just a cat, but Konrad Spellman would not. And if they added up all the conversations she had overheard... She shivered, despite the warmth of the summer night.

She made herself walk on. *She* was not a coward.

Footsteps. Behind her. They broke into a run.

She tensed, heart pounding, mouth dry.

"Cat! Wait!" A familiar voice. Garth's voice. A moment later, he drew up beside her, panting.

"Thank Freyn I caught up with you. I didn't think you'd

go by yourself. Cat, you mustn't. Look, if you really want me to go, I will. But listen to my plan first. Please."

He did care. She stopped and listened.

# MIDSUMMER NIGHT

THE CITY BLAZED WITH LIGHT AND LIFE and laughter. As the day softened into dusk and the lamps were lit, people, dressed in their best silks, or their best homespun, burst into the streets to eat, to drink, to talk, to sing, to dance, or just to watch. For tonight was Midsummer, and all Freya celebrated.

Garth dodged out of the way of a cartwheeling acrobat, only to be caught at the edge of revellers kicking up their heels to a merry jig. Behind them, a group of men bellowed out the words of a drinking song. From the corner of her eye, Cat saw an arc of torches flash and wheel with magical grace around a juggler's head.

Konrad had left the house hours earlier. The wizards were to meet the queen and each other over dinner. The musicians had been instructed to arrive shortly after nightfall. Despite Garth's protests, Annette had insisted he eat before he left. Cat was glad no one had made her eat. Her stomach felt like a wriggling worm.

They turned a corner. At the far end of the square, the palace glittered like a diamond ringed by lesser gems. Or like a spider in the middle of its web, Cat thought. She shivered.

A crowd stood in the square at a respectful distance from the line of soldiers on guard. People craned their heads for a sight of Queen Elira or any of the famous wizards who were there. Cat's eyes flew from face to face.

Lianna and Kenton weren't hard to find. They stood slightly to one side, and, unlike the others, they were still, their eyes fixed on those approaching the palace.

Cat saw Lianna start and move forward before she spied Gayland. He was strolling up the street a short distance ahead of them. Dressed in bright red and yellow, with a matching cap on his head, he looked as gay and jaunty as any carefree reveller. Even the satchel on his back in which he, like Garth, carried his lute, was the colour of sunshine.

Lianna seized Gayland's arm. Cat was too far back to hear what she said, but she saw Gayland's surprise as he turned and recognized Lianna, saw the urgency in Lianna's face as she spoke, the shock on her father's, the slow shake of his head, the bitter disappointment that filled her mother.

Gayland placed a hand on Lianna's shoulder. He opened his mouth as though to speak, then closed it, bereft of words for once. He patted Lianna's shoulder, then dropped his hand and turned away. Lianna's head was bowed.

Garth's eyes had followed Cat's. He looked from Gayland to Lianna, then down at Cat, trembling in his arms. His eyes were wide. "Your mother?" he whispered. Cat nodded.

"Oh, Cat, I'm sorry. I'm so sorry."

His words warmed the cold hollow inside her – a little. But Garth mustn't be distracted. He must concentrate. This spell couldn't go wrong. Resolutely, she looked away from her mother.

"I could tell her."

She shook her head.

He hesitated, then sighed and moved on.

In front of the palace, Garth was stopped by a young, stern-faced soldier who demanded his name, searched him thoroughly, and frowned at Cat. "You can't take that animal inside."

He was overheard by another guard. "It's all right, Shepherd. Captain Penner left word that Garth Spellman was to be allowed to take his cat in with him."

So Konrad Spellman had kept his word and spoken to the captain. Why? What did the wizard know? What did he plan?

A servant led them up a flight of stairs so richly carpeted with a royal blue rug that feet made no sound. The ornately carved banister gleamed with polish.

A hum of voices grew louder the higher they climbed. Cat's heart raced when she saw the massive double doors at the top of the stairs, guarded by two soldiers standing at rigid attention. The servant led them past the doors to a small antechamber.

Three people already sat there. Cat saw Talisa, looking

like some rare, lovely flower with her pale face, shining red hair, and green gown that was a perfect match for her long-lashed eyes. But Cat spared her only one glance before her attention switched to Gayland.

He was frowning, his carefree air dropped like a discarded cloak. He glanced up briefly and nodded at Garth, but his mind was clearly elsewhere.

He was worried. Worried about her.

*I will protect him. No matter what, I will protect him.*

Garth removed his pack, then sat down on one of the tapestried chairs. Cat sat by his feet. The last musician entered. They waited. No one spoke.

A short, balding man appeared in the doorway. Cat recognized him as one of the judges, though his clothes had changed from sober black broadcloth to rich purple satin.

"Good, you're all here," he said, looking around. "In a few minutes, we'll go in. To be fair, I'll draw names to determine who will go in what order."

There was a rustle of anticipation, a plucking of strings as the musicians tuned their instruments. Garth's hands shook as he did so. Then it was time.

Cat was very conscious of watching eyes as she walked down the long length of the polished hall and took her place beside Garth's chair. There was a flash of green as Talisa seated herself beside them.

The faces in front of her were a blur. She forced herself to focus on them.

Queen Elira, a golden diadem adorning her auburn hair, sat in the centre of the front row. On her right was a man

Cat remembered from the day of the queen's arrival, her cousin, Count Varic. Cat's eyes went to his hands, resting on the arms of his chair. Sure enough, they were both heavily adorned with rings. To the queen's left was a middle-aged man with bushy eyebrows, dressed in black. Cat's eyes scanned more faces, came to rest on one she recognized. Kerstin Brooks. Beside her sat a man with dark eyes, a mobile face, and curly grey hair. Next to him – Cat's breath caught – was Konrad Spellman, steadily regarding his grandson. As though aware of her gaze, he glanced at Cat. She looked away.

She felt other eyes on her and darted a glance their way. The plump, pink-cheeked Islandian woman who had stared at Cat down at the harbour was staring at her again, as at some intriguing puzzle. She knows, Cat thought again. She knows I'm not a cat. But the Islandian represented no present danger. Cat's gaze moved on.

She spied Master Wishbe, then a woman who was an older version of Talisa, then, like a breath of home air, Master Weaver.

There must have been sixty or seventy people in the hall: courtiers, black-robed teachers from the College of Wizards, other Freyan wizards, a handful of Islandians, and perhaps a dozen Uglessians. Guards stood discreetly along the walls. Cat's attention froze on the tall, broad-shouldered figure of Captain Penner. There was no sign of the knife.

She was so absorbed in watching the captain that she jumped when she heard the rippling notes of a harp. Dragging her thoughts away from the soldier, she focused on the first musician, a man with an eagle's beak of a nose. His song held echoes of an old wayfarers' tune, one well chosen, Cat thought, for his words told the story of three strangers – Freya, Uglessia, and Islandia – meeting on the road, and of suspicion and hostility turning into a friendship that allowed them to continue the journey with their strength multiplied threefold. The man's voice was deep and resonant, and his song ended to thunderous applause.

Cat waited, breathing quickly, to hear who would be next.

"Talisa Thatcher."

The Uglessian sang without musical accompaniment. Her voice was pure and achingly beautiful. Better than mine, Cat realized. Much better. Envy stirred. She thrust it down. There was no time for that tonight.

Talisa sang in Uglessian, but there could be little doubt about the meaning of her words, and no doubt about the joy that filled her voice and resounded through the room. Again, applause rang out.

"Garth Spellman."

Cat heard Garth gulp. It doesn't matter, she told herself. What matters is that we're here, that we have a chance to stop the plot and save my father's life. That's all that matters. Nevertheless, she closed her eyes and sent a quick, fervent prayer to Freyn.

It worked. Or, at least, something worked. Garth's voice was true, his words emerged with passion and precision, and his lute caught the complex rhythms of Freyfall and the simple, clear melody of Mab.

The hush that greeted his song was even better than the claps and cheers that followed.

Garth resumed his seat, face flushed, eyes shining. Talisa leaned towards him. "That was beautiful," she murmured. Garth stammered his thanks. "So was yours."

A mutual admiration society, Cat thought sourly. Her elation dimmed.

"Gayland Bellmore," the judge announced, and suddenly nothing else counted.

She cast a quick glance at Garth. He sat stiffly upright, his gaze fixed on her father. Would he remember the spell? Would he cast it correctly? He had spent long hours learning it, bending over yellowed pages in a book in his grandfather's study while Cat kept watch. But he was flustered, excited by his success. And he *did* make mistakes. She should know.

She waited, heart thudding painfully, while Gayland took his position and played the opening notes. The timing had to be right. She knew that. Garth had explained that it took a couple of minutes for the magic to take hold, and that its effects lasted for only a short duration. But as Gayland began singing in his smooth, polished voice, panic clogged her throat. She tapped Garth's leg. He looked down and shook his head.

It wasn't until Gayland finished the second verse that Garth started the spell. Cat couldn't hear his words, but she saw his lips move. She could only pray that his words were correct, his timing accurate.

The dance refrain, introducing Uglessia. Third verse. The gentle, opening notes of the lullaby.

*And when evening ends and night's shadows fall*

It wasn't working. Wouldn't work. If it did take hold, it wouldn't be soon enough.

Cat's eyes swung to Captain Penner. He hadn't moved, but she noticed that he stood poised, his right leg slightly in advance of his left. A snake, ready to strike. She tensed.

Then, suddenly, the words stopped making sense. The melody continued, beautiful, hauntingly familiar. But the words were as meaningless as though they were sung in a nonsensical language known only to the singer. Cat saw the faces across from her go blank.

The song ended with deep, mournful notes that were a shocking contrast to the joyful lyricism and peace that preceded them. Cat watched bewilderment deepen on the faces of the people in the room as they heard what sounded remarkably like the tolling of the death bell.

Gayland raised his hand from the lute and gave a dramatic bow. Cat wondered, with a tug at her heart, if he expected this to be his final bow.

There was a short pause, then polite claps. Gayland looked as bewildered as a man might who expects to awaken a hornet's nest and finds himself among a flutter of butterflies instead.

The judge stepped forward, his face expressionless, and cleared his throat. "The last performer is –"

"Excuse me," said a voice Cat knew. Master Wishbe's voice. "I failed to catch the final stanzas. I think others did as well." He shot a baleful glance at Gayland. "Perhaps Master

Bellmore could repeat his song – more clearly this time."

"Please. The rest of it was so delightful, it would be a shame not to hear its conclusion," said another man, one dressed in yellow silk. His smile was, Cat thought, as false as the ones Aunt Dalia gave her.

The judge hesitated, then looked to the queen for direction.

Queen Elira frowned. "We agree that the tune was lovely. However, the night is drawing on, and we have urgent business to conduct come morning. We should proceed."

"Your judgement, as always, shows great wisdom." This came from the man sitting beside the queen. Her cousin, Count Varic. He displayed even white teeth in a smile that could have charmed wild birds from their trees. "Still, I agree with the worthy Master Wishbe and Lord Fairtree. It would be a woeful shame to miss hearing such a moving song in its entirety. If the good musician could repeat the last three verses only, we would not be long delayed."

Murmurs of agreement came from around the room.

Queen Elira sat very still for a moment. Then she said, "Very well," and nodded to Gayland. "Proceed."

Looking like a man who'd lost his way in the fog, Gayland started to raise his lute. He stopped and glanced quickly at Garth, eyes narrowed in sudden suspicion.

Cat looked at Garth too. The boy's face was white. His lips moved silently. But Cat knew, as surely as though Garth had spoken aloud, that there was no hope. There was no time for the spell to take effect.

The words rang clearly in the quiet room.

*And when evening ends and night's shadows fall*
*The spirits keep their watch over one and all*
*They guard the slumbers, but find it hard to tell*
*Which dreams come from people and which from ursells.*

*And now we are joining our minds and hearts*
*And here we are sharing in our magic arts*
*The knowledge of Freya, the wisdom of the west*
*The instincts of the beast, by the spirits blessed.*

Cat heard gasps, startled cries. Gayland's voice soared above them.

*For who's man and who's beast when dressed in ursell grey?*
*Who can tell the difference by what they do or say?*
*So here's to our union, of mind and heart and — smell*
*Let's sing on our path till the tolling of the bell.*

Again, the death bell tolled.

By the time the last chord died away, clamorous shouts of outrage filled the room. Not that anyone could understand the shouts: Garth's spell had finally taken hold.

Cat gave one quick look around before heading towards Captain Penner. In that glance, she detected a small smile on Count Varic's face before it was replaced by shocked disgust. Master Wishbe also wore a mask of horror. But Konrad Spellman was staring at his grandson, and as for the Uglessians.... Cat didn't understand. They appeared neither shocked nor angry, merely...interested.

Like spectators at a cockfight.

She had no time to wonder about them. Too many people were up and moving, calling, gesturing, creating chaos. And Captain Penner was striding towards the hubbub.

Cat felt conspicuous as she streaked across the front of the hall, but surely no one noticed her. Most eyes were on Gayland.

The magic lifted, like morning mist. The cries were clear.

"Outrageous!"

"How dare you?"

"An insult to us all."

"How could the queen's judges approve that song?" someone asked loudly.

"They must have been duped," a man retorted. Other voices from all around the room were apologizing to the Uglessians. Cat still hadn't heard them say anything.

Then someone near the front laughed. "You must admit," a languid voice drawled, "it was funny. And appropriate."

Cat spared a glance over her shoulder, and saw a fair-haired young man, dressed in maroon satin, throw back his head and laugh. His laughter killed the clamour as effectively as the announcement of death the merriment at a wedding.

"That was uncalled for, Lord Dalemark," Queen Elira said coldly.

Her rebuke came too late. Past the sea of legs, Cat saw a tall young Uglessian jump to his feet.

"Funny? What do you mean, funny?" His voice shook

with fury. He took one long stride forward.

"Thannis," a woman said softly. Warningly. The young man stopped.

"Amusing, wouldn't you say?" Lord Dalemark asked. "Quite a comic picture it brought to mind."

Was the man totally stupid? Or was he part of the conspiracy? How many people here tonight were involved?

An older Uglessian was on his feet. He put a restraining hand on Thannis's arm.

Then someone else, close to the queen's chair, laughed. It was the man in yellow silk who'd requested a repetition of Gayland's song earlier.

With a roar of rage, Thannis threw off the hand and lunged towards the laughter. Those in his path dodged out of his way. A frail old man put out an arm to stop him. Without looking, Thannis brushed it aside. The man tottered and fell, knocking over his chair. A wizard leapt out of the way of the chair and bumped into another, sending it and its occupant to the ground.

Where was Captain Penner? She had allowed herself to be distracted.

Then she heard his voice. "Make way." She breathed a sigh of relief and darted around a russet-coloured skirt and between a pair of black-clad legs.

There he was, tall, commanding in his green uniform, clearing a trail before him like a vigorous broom cleaning a room.

Cat moved forward. She would stick to him like a leech. If he approached her father...

But he wasn't approaching him. He was heading straight towards the group around the queen. So was Thannis. Soldiers were pushing their way through the crowd, converging on the Uglessian. There were too many of them. People trying to get out of their way bumped into other soldiers.

Noise. So much noise it hurt her ears. Shouts. Curses, as wizards and courtiers were shoved aside or stumbled into each other. Words that sounded like spells. If they were, they didn't seem to be working. Or perhaps different spells cancelled each other out.

She had a clear view of Queen Elira now. The queen was on her feet, her eyes sparking with anger. Count Varic stood close to her. So did Master Wishbe and another wizard, dressed in College black, the man in yellow silk, and Lord Dalemark in his maroon satin.

Gayland remained in the same place he'd been in since his performance ended. Four soldiers hovered nearby, but aside from them he stood in lonely isolation. Or not isolation, Cat saw with a sudden catch of her breath. Garth was beside him.

Thannis, his gaze fixed on Lord Dalemark, had almost reached his target.

Count Varic said loudly, "This is disgraceful! You really must make sure you have better judges for your next competition, my dear cousin. Judges who don't hate Uglessians."

Two more strides, and Thannis arrived at the circle around Queen Elira. He grabbed the young man's maroon shirt in one large, six-fingered hand.

Then Captain Penner was there too. He reached for

Thannis with his right hand. But his left hand, hidden from view by the bodies surrounding the queen, stole beneath his tunic.

The knife. He was going for the knife.

But why? He was supposed to use it on Gayland, and Gayland was nowhere near.

She didn't understand, but it didn't matter.

She crouched. Sprang. Landed on his arm. Dug her front claws into his hand and sank her teeth into the soft flesh of his wrist.

# PLOTS & COUNTERPLOTS

CAPTAIN PENNER CRIED OUT.
　　Releasing Thannis, he hit Cat.
　　Pain. Red-hot. Searing. All of Cat's instincts screamed at her to let go. She didn't. She dug in deeper.

His large right hand grabbed her, tried to pull her off. She closed her eyes, as though that would shut out the pain. Leechlike, she burrowed down. Blood filled her mouth.

He tore at her. She felt fur loosen. Wrench away.

His hand clenched around her neck. She couldn't breathe. Couldn't...

*Air. She needed air. She must let go.*

She wouldn't. She wouldn't. She *wouldn't*.

He was killing her.

Footsteps. Barked commands.

Then his hand was gone from her throat. She opened her eyes.

Red mist swirled before her. She shut her eyes. Opened them again.

She was surrounded. Surrounded by soldiers. Panic ran like fire through her veins.

No. Wait. One soldier held Captain Penner's arms in a viselike grip. Others pinioned Count Varic, Master Wishbe, all the men who clustered around the queen. Only Thannis stood free, blinking rapidly, like a man waking abruptly from a wild dream.

Count Varic's ring-encrusted fingers tore at the hands of his two captors. "What do you think you're doing?" he spat. "Don't you know who I am?"

Queen Elira rounded on him. "The question is not who you are, but what you have done – or tried to do, my dear cousin." Her voice shook with barely suppressed rage.

Cat saw the count open his mouth, twice, then close it, wordless.

She felt hands trying to lift her. She would not be lifted. Claws and teeth went deeper. Captain Penner jerked and swore.

Behind her, a voice spoke. "You did a good job, but you can let go now." Konrad Spellman's voice. She went rigid.

"Garth, come and call her off," the wizard said.

More footsteps. Then Garth said, close to her ear, "It's all right, Cat. I...I don't understand, but I think we're safe now. Everyone's safe."

Garth put his hands around her. She released her grip and allowed him to lift her from her prey, the taste of blood metallic in her mouth.

"Take them away," Queen Elira ordered.

"Your Majesty, I must protest. We have done nothing to warrant this treatment," Master Wishbe said.

"Your actions tonight indicate otherwise. So does Master Spellman's testimony."

*Master Spellman's testimony? What did the queen mean?*

"Spellman?" Master Wishbe stared at the queen for a moment, then whirled to face the other wizard. "You...you traitor!"

"Just who is the traitor here?" Konrad Spellman asked softly.

"Take them away," Queen Elira repeated. Her eyes fell on Gayland, standing alone in the middle of the floor. "Also the musician."

Gayland's mouth twisted into a rueful smile.

*No! Oh no!* Cat's claws sank instinctively into Garth's arm.

"No!" Garth cried.

Queen Elira looked at him coldly.

He gulped and clutched Cat more tightly. "I mean... please don't, Your Majesty. He didn't know."

"Didn't know? Didn't know that his song insulted our guests? Didn't know that it might destroy goodwill between us and our neighbours?"

Garth was silent. Queen Elira started to turn away.

*Say something, Garth. Say something. Oh, why can't I speak?*

"He didn't know that the knife was meant for you. He thought he was the one to be killed," Garth said.

"We all thought that," his grandfather said. "I am deeply sorry, Your Majesty. My lack of understanding put your life in jeopardy."

"They couldn't trust you with that secret, Kon," said a new voice. Cat twisted her head to see the newcomer, the man with curly grey hair and mobile face. Kerstin Brooks stood beside him. "They thought you'd join a plot to discredit the Uglessians, but knew you'd never condone an attempt to assassinate the queen."

"An attempt that might have succeeded had the cat not intervened," Kerstin said, smiling down at Cat. She turned to the queen. "Might I suggest we adjourn to another room? It seems to me there are mysteries here – mysteries of a speech-scrambling spell, mysteries of this cat's actions. May I also suggest that the musician accompany us?"

Queen Elira hesitated, then nodded curtly. "A good idea. Please ask representatives from the Islandian and Uglessian delegations to join us. Meanwhile –" she took a deep breath – "we will apologize to our guests and ask them to reassemble in the morning."

"Excuse me," Garth said. All eyes swung to him. He swallowed. "There are two people outside who should be present. May I ask them to join us if they're willing?"

The queen looked irritated, but nodded. "Very well."

She turned to speak to the gawking, bewildered assembly, but Cat didn't hear what Queen Elira said. She and Garth were hurrying towards the door.

THEY WERE STILL THERE. When Garth dashed up to them and asked them to go with him, they stared at him as though he were playing some senseless Midsummer joke.

"It concerns Cat," Garth said. "And Gayland."

Lianna gasped. "Cat? Do you know where she is?"

Garth nodded.

"Is...is she...?"

"She's fine," Garth assured her. "But Gayland's in trouble."

Lianna and Kenton looked at each other, then followed Garth without another word.

The guards were jumpy and suspicious, having just seen their captain led away by others of their kind, but Garth drew himself up and announced that he had the queen's own permission to bring these two inside.

Konrad Spellman was waiting for them at the foot of the stairs. He glanced curiously at Lianna and Kenton, but all he said was, "This way."

"Grandfather –" Garth began.

"Later. We must not keep Queen Elira waiting."

The room he led them to was no less formal than the grand hall, but much smaller. It seemed crowded, even though only eight people sat on the stiff chairs upholstered in blue and silver brocade. Cat's eyes went immediately to Gayland.

He looked very alone somehow – alone and vulnerable, despite his jaunty red and yellow garments. He glanced up idly when the newcomers entered, then sprang to his feet.

"Lianna! What are you doing here?"

"It's all right. Really it is," Garth said hastily.

Gayland shot him a scorching glare. "You! Interfering again. You had no right to drag her into this. She's done nothing wrong."

"We're not in any danger, Gayland," Lianna said quietly. "We're here because this boy said he knew where Cat is, and that you're in trouble."

"Please take your seats," the queen said impatiently. "There is much to discuss, and the night is drawing on. Your names?"

Kenton bowed. "My name is Kenton Herd, and this is my wife Lianna." Lianna curtseyed. They sat. Neither seemed overwhelmed by the company. Cat was proud of them.

"You obviously know Gayland Bellmore, who is an accomplished musician, but with whose sense of humour we have a grave quarrel."

Gayland inclined his head.

"To our right are Jem Brooks and his wife Kerstin, better known to the world as Kerstin Speller."

Lianna's eyes widened. Kenton frankly stared.

"To her right are Morena, who serves as Speaker for the Circle in Islandia, and Raven, the Islandian Healer."

Islandian Healer! Cat's eyes fastened on the lean face of the man with a shock of white in his night-black hair. He and his companion, an elderly woman with a weathered face and sharp, dark eyes, nodded their greeting. Cat looked away reluctantly as the queen continued her introductions.

"On our left are Redelle Thatcher and her husband Alaric from Uglessia."

The woman with an older version of Talisa's face smiled. The man, who had iron-grey hair above a fine-featured face, nodded.

"Last, but not least, are Konrad Spellman, a noted Freyan wizard, and his grandson, whose name, we are told, is Garth."

"And who is, I suspect, a noted wizard himself." Kerstin Brooks leaned forward. "It *was* you who cast the scrambling spell, was it not?" she asked Garth.

He flushed. "Yes."

"Why?"

"Why? Well, we...I found out about the conspiracy and...well, I couldn't think of any other way to stop it."

"Why not just report it?" the queen demanded.

Garth glanced sideways at his grandfather, then studied the blue and silver rug beneath his feet. "I..." He stopped.

"He thought I was involved," Konrad said.

Garth raised his head and looked at the wizard. "I'm sorry, Grandfather. I'm so sorry. I should have known."

"Why?" his grandfather asked mildly. "Danlo Wishbe and his fellow conspirators believed I was one with them, after all, and there was a time when my hatred of Uglessians almost led to Redelle's death." He smiled at the red-haired Uglessian. "Even after that, it took some time for my suspicions to disappear completely. My father had trained me all too well. But how should you know that? It has occurred to me, this last while, that I have rarely confided my thoughts and feelings to you."

"But —"

"I told Wishbe that I was with them so that I could learn as much as possible about the plot. I even swore a sacred oath." The wizard's mouth tightened. "I sent word secretly to Queen Elira, and when Jem arrived in town, I asked him to alert the Uglessians and Islandians so that trouble wouldn't erupt."

"Even so, that fool Thannis lost his head," Redelle said.

"To do him justice, he *did* heed our warning," her husband pointed out. "We had told him not to attack the singer, no matter what the provocation. How was he to know that a fight near the queen would lead to disaster?"

"He could have thought," Redelle said tartly.

"I knew Danlo was keeping a lot from me, including the names of many of the conspirators," Konrad continued. "We decided to let the evening proceed as planned. Give the conspirators rope enough to hang themselves."

"I nearly wrecked your plans," Garth said miserably.

"No," Queen Elira said. She smiled at him. "Your spell forced our cousin out into the open. Without it, we would never have known about his involvement. We are not totally surprised, however. He's always been ambitious, and he's never been in favour of our policy towards Uglessia."

"Danlo said we had friends in high places, but he never named them," Konrad confirmed. "We had to move cautiously, not knowing who was in on the plot." He sighed. "We tried to make sure of the guards in the hall tonight. Some were Penner's men. We didn't dare confide in them. But others we could trust. They were ready to move as soon as Penner took a step towards Bellmore. What I didn't understand was that Bellmore wasn't the target. The night could have ended in disaster."

"It would have if it weren't for Cat," Garth said proudly, glancing down at Cat, who sat alertly by his chair. A tide of warmth flowed through her. It almost thawed the fear that had chilled her since the queen ordered Gayland's arrest.

Garth looked back at his grandfather. "All the same, I should have known you weren't a traitor. Please forgive me."

Konrad was silent for a moment before he said slowly, "I must admit that I was hurt when it became obvious to me that you knew at least a little about the plot, but didn't trust me enough to tell me. But then something else became clear. You weren't going to tell *anyone* about it, but you were trying very hard to find some way to stop it. Why?"

"Why? Well...I had to stop it. If it had worked, the results could have been... I had to stop it."

"Then why not tell someone?"

"I couldn't!" Garth exclaimed. "I couldn't put you in danger." He hesitated, then said softly, "I love you."

His grandfather smiled, a smile that transformed his face like sun emerging from cloud. Watching him, Cat wondered why she had been so afraid of this man.

"There's nothing to forgive," he said quietly.

There was a long pause, broken by Queen Elira. "Now that the events of this evening have been explained, and we have caught all the troublemakers –"

"Excuse me, Your Majesty," Jem Brooks interrupted. He was frowning thoughtfully. "Ever since I heard about this conspiracy, I've wondered why those involved were so sure that Bellmore would be chosen as one of the winners. Not that your song wasn't good, of course," he assured the musician. Gayland bowed his head in acknowledgement. "But how could they be *sure?*"

"You're implying that our musicians are corrupt?" the queen asked sharply.

"I think they should be investigated," the wizard said.

"We were broken into groups for the trials," Garth said. "Maybe only the one who heard Gayland first knew anything about it. The conspirators may have felt confident that he could convince the others if they needed convincing."

After a moment, Queen Elira nodded. "Very well. We will have him questioned. There may well be others in the plot." Her lips tightened. "However, that can wait for now. For tonight, we need only decide what is to be done with this man." She gave Gayland a look she might have given a cockroach. "Then we can retire for the night."

Warmth evaporated. A cold hand grasped Cat's stomach and twisted. In the chair beside her, Lianna stirred uneasily.

"You must pardon him," Garth said earnestly.

"Indeed? And why must we do that?"

"He meant you no harm. Truly, Your Majesty. And he bears Uglessians no ill will. He only agreed to write his song because he needed money. His wife is sick and –"

"And so he turned traitor. You are asking us to pardon him out of pity?"

Gayland straightened. "I ask for no pity. I did what I did and will suffer the consequences."

"At least you have courage," the queen said. "But you are quite right. You *will* suffer the consequences."

"No!" Garth cried.

Everyone looked at him. His grandfather shook his head.

"No," Garth repeated. "You must pardon him. If for no other reason, you must pardon him because his daughter saved your life."

# SPELLS & COUNTERSPELLS

"DAUGHTER?" GAYLAND ECHOED. "STOP speaking in riddles, boy."

"But it was the cat that –" Kerstin Brooks stopped in mid-sentence and stared at Cat.

Lianna turned on Garth, fists clenched. "What do you mean, Gayland's daughter saved the queen? You keep talking about Cat. You said you knew where she is. Now you say... Where is she? Where is my daughter?" Her voice rose, trembled on the edge of hysteria.

Garth gulped. "Here."

"Here?" Lianna's body shook like someone in a high fever. "How can you... Where is she?"

"She's...I transformed her. By mistake. She's...well, she's the cat."

Lianna stared at him, then at Cat. There was nothing on her face but shock. Disbelief.

*It is me. It is. It is. Please. Please believe. I'm here. I'm me.*

"Look. Her fur's the same tawny colour as Cat's hair," Kenton said softly.

"Yes," Lianna whispered. "Yes, it... Oh, Cat." She bent down, touched Cat tentatively. Then she gathered her in her arms and buried her face in Cat's fur. Cat snuggled closer.

"So that's it," Gayland said. "The cat. The cat who loves music, who brought you to us, who I've seen so often. But how? Why? Why did you turn my daughter into a cat?"

"It was an accident."

Alaric Thatcher's lips twitched. "Quite an accident. Transformation spells are beyond the power of most wizards."

"Especially those who don't even know them," Konrad added. He shook his head. "I couldn't believe it when I first began to suspect. How could you have changed her? But the more I saw the two of you together, the more I realized there was more to this cat than just fur and claws. I wasn't really sure, though. Not till now."

"I couldn't have done it on purpose," Garth said apologetically. "Cat came to me for a finding spell when she was searching for her father. Somehow I...well, I got the words mixed up."

"But the two are as far apart as Freyfall and Frey-by-the-Sea," Kerstin said.

"Are they? I didn't know. I can't even remember what I said. I did try to find the transformation spell so I could reverse it, but it's in Grandfather's locked book and I don't know how to unlock it."

"Just as well," Konrad said dryly.

"I suppose," Garth said humbly. "I was going to tell you when you returned home, Grandfather, really I was, but Cat stopped me."

"Hardly surprising, since she'd just overheard a highly treasonable conversation between Wishbe and myself. Well, better late than never."

Lianna looked up. "You can turn her back into herself?"

Konrad nodded.

Cat sat up straight on Lianna's lap. *At last. At last to be a girl again.* She listened carefully as the wizard began. She didn't understand the words, but she felt power tremble in the air. She trembled too, and closed her eyes. *Soon. Soon.*

The words stopped. The room was silent.

It was strange. She didn't feel different. Shouldn't she feel different? Shouldn't the smells in the air, the sounds in the room, have changed?

She opened her eyes. Looked down. Saw fur, paws, Lianna's grey dress.

The silence stretched on and on.

"It didn't work," Gayland said.

"No." Konrad rubbed a hand across his eyes. "Maybe I did something wrong." For the first time, Cat heard a note of uncertainty in his voice.

"No," Kerstin said. "Everything was correct." She looked thoughtfully at Garth. "What exactly did you do when you placed the spell?"

"I...I don't know," he stammered. "I said the words of the finding spell and focused on a tin whistle that had belonged to Cat's father."

"My old whistle!" Gayland exclaimed. He looked at Cat. "You kept it all these years," he said softly.

She nodded. Somewhere, distantly, she was glad he was pleased. But that meant little. Everything meant little except the rising tide of panic that threatened to drown her.

Lianna stroked her gently.

"And?" Kerstin demanded.

"I tried to concentrate, but Gayland's impression on the whistle was faint. Pictures of Cat, playing it by a small brook or in a meadow, kept sliding in front. I knew the spell wasn't working, so I repeated it. Or I thought I did."

"Do you remember what you were thinking?"

"Thinking? Well, I know I was worried that I would fail, and wishing I were a better wizard, for her sake."

"Anything else?"

Garth looked at the floor. "Not really. I guess...I was sort of listening in my mind to the music she had played. And...well, I was thinking how pretty she was. I remember wishing I knew her name."

"She hadn't told you?"

"No."

Kerstin glanced at Lianna. "I think you called your daughter Cat. Is that her name?"

"It's really Catrina, but everyone calls her Cat."

The wizard looked back at Garth. "You called her Cat. Why?"

"I don't...it just felt right, somehow. Then I found out from her father that her name was Catrina."

Alaric leaned forward. "You don't think he used a

naming spell, do you, Kerstin?"

She nodded. "It would fit."

Redelle frowned. "I have never heard of this."

"It's very old, and never used these days. Wizards used to believe that a person's essence was captured in his or her name. They devised this spell to discover people's names. Alaric and I only know about it because Father had a collection of books about the ancient history of wizardry. As I recall, the words are very similar to those of the finding spell. If Garth reversed a couple, or mispronounced them, while wondering about her name and holding her whistle, he might have evoked the naming spell. Magic is formed at least as much by wizards' hearts and intentions as by their words, after all."

"I don't see how just naming her Cat could turn her into one," Konrad objected.

Kerstin pushed a strand of hair from her forehead. "It seems unlikely," she admitted. "Still, if the ancient wizards were right and names *do* hold a person's essence – though that theory has fallen into disrepute, I confess."

"There's a ballad," Gayland said. Everyone stared at him. "It's an old one, about a mighty wizard who pursued a beautiful young woman called Willow. She would have nothing to do with him, so he sought to gain power over her by finding her name. The spell he used in order to do so changed her into a graceful willow tree. The song says she still weeps for her lost self." Gayland looked around the circle. "I won't swear there's truth in a ballad, but there might be. And if it happened once…"

"I wonder," Alaric said slowly. "Many old spells have been suppressed because they were too powerful and too dangerous. If –"

"Talk!" Kenton burst out. "All this talk, as though this were all just *theory*. What does *theory* matter? What matters is Cat. Can anyone turn her back into herself?"

Kerstin frowned. "I don't know. If a naming spell *does* capture a person's essence, then to reverse it –" Her eyes moved to Cat, then away.

Lianna's hands held Cat tightly, but even that didn't stop the tremors shaking her.

"I am sorry." It was the elderly Islandian woman, speaking in slow, heavily accented Freyan. "Neither Raven nor I have understood all you have said. Will someone explain?"

Kerstin opened her mouth, then shook her head. "It's complicated. Perhaps it would be best if you looked into my mind."

The woman smiled. "Good."

Look into her mind? Cat's breath caught. If Islandians had the power to do such things, then surely... Hope fluttered in her heart.

The room was quiet. The old woman's face was intent. Listening. Candlelight glowed in her dark eyes.

She nodded. "Thank you." She turned to the man. The Healer. Raven. Something silent passed between them.

Queen Elira leaned forward. "We have heard much of the strong magic possessed by those who live within the Circle in Islandia. Are you able to lift the enchantment from this girl?"

The two Islandians exchanged a glance. Then the woman said, "No." Her eyes rested on Cat. "Our magic is too different. I am sorry."

Someone groaned. Garth, Cat thought. She wasn't sure. She was falling down a bottomless pit. But there was a bottom, she knew. She would hit it and know, finally, without the possibility of hope or release, that she was trapped in a cat's body forever.

"Perhaps the person who cast the spell should reverse it," Jem suggested.

Garth gasped. "Me?"

"Yes. It seems you're the only one alive who's ever made a naming spell, intentionally or not. And none of us – at least none of us who have studied wizardry – know Cat as you do."

"But I don't know it! I'd never even heard about it until tonight. I can't –"

"Kerstin has read it. She never forgets the words of a spell. She can teach them to you. You know how to reverse spells, don't you?"

"Yes, but –"

"Then reverse this one. And while you do, think of the pictures you saw of the girl playing her whistle by the stream and in the meadow. Wish for that girl to appear, as intently as you wished to find her name."

Cat's eyes moved from face to face. There were frowns, but they were thoughtful frowns. Then Kerstin nodded. Redelle smiled.

Were they right? Hope stirred again, feeble but present.

Garth's face was ashen. "I can't."

"Why not?" his grandfather asked.

"I'm not a wizard. I'm an apprentice, and not even a good one. You know that. I might harm her. Look what I did last time."

"You *are* a wizard," Konrad said. "A good one, when you pay attention. You can do it. Try."

Garth closed his eyes, then opened them and stared at Cat. She stared back.

She was frightened. So frightened. But so was Garth, and Garth needed to be calm. Needed to feel confident.

When she was ten, her cousin had dared her to eat an eel. She had forced her revulsion down, forced a smile onto her face. It was like that now, forcing her fear down, forcing her body to be still. Not to tremble. Not to shake.

*You can do it, Garth. You can. I trust you.*

"All right," Garth said.

Cat shut her eyes. "Picture her," Jem had said. She too made a picture, held it, even though the fear kept trying to push it aside. A picture of herself, sitting on a flat rock beside the brook at Ashdale Farm. *See it, Garth. See it as I see it. See me.*

She heard Kerstin recite words, heard Garth repeat them softly. Then, after a minute, he spoke again, slowly, firmly. She didn't listen. She concentrated on the picture. She was in the picture. She could feel the granite beneath her, warmed by the sun, feel the soft breeze that touched her hair.

Peace. She was at home. She was safe. She was –

Spinning. Tilting. Or was it the world, shifting, out of balance?

She opened her eyes. Saw hands. Arms. Naked arms.

She was a girl. A naked girl. And much too large for her mother's lap. She tumbled to the floor, landing on all fours. A moment later, she felt a cloak drop lightly on her. She looked up, dazed.

It was Kenton's cloak. He was smiling. But Lianna's face was wet with tears. "Cat. Oh, Cat."

Cat heard exclamations, relieved laughter. She saw Garth's face. It was a pale shade of green. But none of that mattered. She picked herself up, wrapped the cloak tightly around herself, and flung herself into her mother's arms.

# ENDINGS & BEGINNINGS

A SHORT TIME LATER, BATHED AND DRESSED IN Queen Elira's plainest gown, Cat returned to the room, accompanied by Lianna and one of the queen's attendants.

Little had changed. The wizards were still discussing the mystery of the naming spell. Kenton, Gayland, and the Islandians still sat quietly. Queen Elira was reading a report handed her by one of the guards at the door. Only Garth looked different, pale but no longer sickly green. He sprang to his feet when Cat entered.

"You're all right?"

She nodded.

He sighed with relief, then smiled at her, a bit shyly, she thought. "You look the way I remember, only...only different somehow."

She smiled back, very conscious of her hair, still wet from its thorough scrubbing, and the green dress that was just a little too large for her but felt incredibly soft and supple. "Cleaner, I hope."

He laughed, then sobered. "I'm so glad you're a girl again. I don't know what I did, now or earlier, but I'm glad."

"You proved you are a powerful wizard," Konrad said.

"Huh? But I made a terrible mistake."

"You did. But you were only able to make it because you have great power for magic."

"But...I don't understand. You always said –"

"I always said you don't pay attention. I never said you lacked the potential to become a good magician."

"A very good magician," Kerstin affirmed.

"I thought –" Garth stopped and rubbed his forehead as though trying to rub sense into it. Then he looked at his grandfather. "I still want to be a musician."

Konrad was silent.

"I'm sorry. I know... Are you very disappointed?"

"Yes," his grandfather admitted, "though not, I suspect, as disappointed as I would have been a month ago." He looked at his grandson's worried face and smiled faintly. "Don't fret. I'll survive."

Garth's face relaxed. "I'd probably never pay proper attention," he offered. "There'd always be a tune wandering around my head."

"Yes. Well, at least you've proved they'd be good tunes. I'll arrange to have you apprenticed to a master musician. I presume you can advise me on who is best." He hesitated. "Most apprentices live in their master's homes, but –"

"I'd like to live with you and Mother, if I may."

Konrad smiled. "You may indeed." He glanced around the room. "I apologize for taking time over private matters. It is late. I suggest we retire for the night."

"An excellent idea, Master Spellman," Queen Elira said. Small lines of weariness were etched around her eyes.

Konrad looked at Lianna and Kenton. "I trust you and your daughter will spend the night with us."

"We have a place at an inn," Kenton demurred.

"Please stay," Garth pleaded.

"We will, with thanks," Lianna said.

"And my fate?" Gayland asked.

The queen frowned. Cat stiffened. She had forgotten. She had actually forgotten. Gayland was still in danger. She took a step forward and sank into a curtsey. Her legs felt stiff and awkward. But then, her whole body felt awkward. It would take time to readjust to her human form.

"Your Majesty –" Her voice cracked. She took a deep breath and started again. "Your Majesty, please forgive my father."

Queen Elira's frown disappeared. She even smiled slightly. She turned to Gayland. "Go your way. You are pardoned, if only for your daughter's sake. But if we hear of you spreading your song in the streets and taverns, the consequences will be severe."

"I won't. I swear to Freyn I won't," Gayland said earnestly. He bowed deeply.

The black-haired healer from Islandia spoke for the first time, his Freyan slow and accented. "This boy – Garth – he says your wife is sick?"

Gayland's mouth tightened. "Yes. She coughs all the time. Sometimes she coughs up blood. A healer – Master Birchill, his name was – sold us some medicine, but it does little good. He said rest and good food were the best cure."

"Your healer is right. But perhaps I can do something for her." He rose, his lean brown face intent.

Gayland stared at him.

"If anyone can help your wife, Raven can," Kerstin said.

Sudden hope leaped into Gayland's eyes. He turned to go, his face alight. Then he stopped and glanced at Cat.

"Cat? You came to Freyfall to find me. I have been a neglectful father and don't deserve such a daughter, but... Will you live with us, in our new home in Applegarth? Lucia would love to have you, and I...I would be very glad."

"No!" Garth cried. "I mean...you'll stay with us, won't you? You can be apprenticed too. You're a musician."

"You would be most welcome," Konrad said. "My grandson would obviously be happy, and my daughter-in-law, I'm sure, would be pleased. She's always been partial to cats." His lips twitched. Then his eyes narrowed. "It might be interesting to test your potential for magic too. When Garth was reversing his spell, I felt power coming from you."

Beside Cat, Lianna stiffened. "Cat –"

Cat gazed around her. Her father, in his brave red and yellow, was inviting her into his life. Garth, who should be delighting in the course his life was taking, wore a worried frown. His dark eyes begged. Lianna's hands clenched and unclenched. Kenton watched Cat steadily.

She had run away from home because she felt unwanted, unloved. But she wasn't. She was surrounded by love.

"Thank you. Thank you all. But I will go back to Frey-under-Hill to live with my mother and Kenton."

Lianna's breath rushed out in a great sigh of relief. Kenton grinned. She didn't look at Garth.

Gayland smiled ruefully. "I'm disappointed. But I hope you will visit us, now and then."

"I will," Cat promised. She still didn't look at Garth.

Gayland came over and took her by the shoulders. "I feel I've come to know you quite well as a cat. Now I'd like a chance to get to know you as my daughter." He bent and kissed her cheek. "Freyn's blessing on you, child, for all you've done." A moment later, accompanied by the Islandian Healer, he was gone.

Cat watched him go through a mist of tears.

Queen Elira rose. "As Master Spellman observed several minutes ago, it is time we retire. Our thanks to all of you for your help and advice. Special thanks to you, Master Spellman, for your timely warning, and to you, Mistress Ashdale. It is the first time our life has been saved by a cat." She smiled. "We shall see most of you in the morning. Freyn's night to you all." She swept out of the room. The others straggled after her.

CAT COULDN'T SLEEP.

She should have slept. The bed was comfortable and the linen sheets blissfully sensuous. She was tired, to the marrow of her bones, an exhaustion bred by weeks of tension finally released. Even the excitement of the night just past should not have kept her awake.

But there was something she had to do and it couldn't wait.

Cat swung her legs – her human legs – over the side of the bed. Grabbing the dressing gown borrowed from Annette, she wrapped it around herself and groped her way to the door. Too bad she didn't still have cat's eyes. She could use them now.

The darkness pressed in on her as she made her way down the hall to Garth's room. She hesitated outside his door. The house was very still. Was he sleeping?

No. She knew he wasn't. She raised her hand and tapped lightly.

"Who is it?" he called after a moment.

"Cat."

There was a long pause. Then the door opened.

"What are you doing here?"

"I want to talk to you. May I come in?"

"You shouldn't be here." But he stepped aside, letting her in.

She supposed she shouldn't. Things were different now that she was a girl again. But it didn't matter.

"I need to talk to you. To explain. And there isn't much time. We'll be leaving tomorrow or the next day. Anyway, this might be the only opportunity to speak with you alone."

He said nothing.

The curtains were drawn. In the dim moonlight that filtered through them, she could see Garth's silhouette, but not his face.

"Garth, when you asked me to live here, I couldn't say yes. I had left home with things unsettled. Unfinished. I didn't give Kenton a chance. He deserves a chance. I have to live with them." She paused, hunting for the right words.

"It's all right," Garth said tonelessly. "I understand."

"Garth –"

"I guess there's no reason why you *would* want to stay here. This place can't hold many pleasant memories for you. It doesn't matter."

Did he mean that? Did it matter nothing to him? Did *she* matter nothing to him? His voice was expressionless, his face hidden by darkness.

Earlier that night, she had thought herself cared for. Loved, even. She should have known better. She should never have come to Garth's room. She turned to go.

No. She didn't believe his words. She didn't believe it didn't matter. In the short time she'd known him, he had allowed her to see him – *really* see him – far more than he would have allowed the girl Cat to do so. His strength, his doubt, his loyalty, his vulnerability – she knew them all. She could allow him to see *her* too.

"Garth," she said quietly, "my choice isn't permanent."

"What do you mean?"

"I need to go home, to be with my mother and Kenton and my grandparents for a few years. And I guess I still have some growing up to do. But after that…" She paused, considering the kaleidoscope of possibilities open to her. She could use her gift of music, train to be a musician. She could explore her potential gift of magic, as Master Spellman had suggested. She could travel, on her own or with her father in his life as a wandering minstrel.

Among all the possibilities, there were two certainties. She would find a way to help the Mabs of the world, the Cats of the world, living on the streets, homeless, hungry. The other certainty... She smiled.

"After that, if you chance to come looking for me, I'll go with you gladly. And if you don't, I might just come to Freyfall looking for *you.*"

"Using a finding spell?" There was a catch in his voice. Was it laughter? Something else?

"If nothing else works."

He made a sound, part snort, part chuckle. Then he was laughing freely. They both were, as they held each other in an embrace that was both a farewell and a promise.

## ABOUT THE AUTHOR

LINDA SMITH is the author of the popular *Freyan Trilogy* fantasy series, which includes *Wind Shifter, Sea Change,* and *The Turning Time.* Titles from that series were finalists for a number of book awards, and her most recent title, the 2003 picture book, *Sir Cassie to the Rescue,* was highly recommended by CM Magazine. She has also published poetry and short fiction in a number of anthologies and periodicals, and has had her work broadcast on CBC Radio.

Born in Lethbridge, Linda Smith grew up in Alberta, and has lived in Truro, Nova Scotia, Saskatoon, and Boston. Since 1984, she has made her home in Grande Prairie, where she worked as a children's librarian until 2001, and where she continues her writing career.